FERAL DARLING

by

ED DIAMANTE

A **ColdRock** ARTS PRODUCTION

FERAL DARLING

ISBN: 978-1-7379386-0-6 (eBook)
ISBN: 978-1-7379386-2-0 (Audiobook)
ISBN: 978-1-7379386-1-3 (Paperback)
ISBN: 978-1-7379386-3-7 (Hardcover)

Library of Congress Control Number: 2021918706

Any references to historical events, real people, or real places are used fictitiously. Names, characters, and places are products of the author's imagination.

Front cover image by Adobe stock
Book design by Marko Markovic, 5mediadesign

Printed by ColdRock Arts, in the United States of America.

First printing edition 2021

Coldrock Entertainment Arts, Inc.
578 Washington Blvd #1174
Marina del Rey, CA 90292

www.ColdrockArts.com

TO MOTHER

CONTENTS

CHAPTER 1

Her fingers strode the raspy bark of unfamiliar trees as her bare feet pranced about the mountain frost. She traversed uncertainty as she did all else in life, like a bubbly child on a carefree summer day, filled with rosy awe. Perhaps those were bouts of denial in the face of tragedy after tragedy after tragedy. It was how she best coped with her circumstance. Even as she again fled death amid that starry, near-moonless night, lost and shrouded in only a crimson cloak.

Illumed or not, Mother Nature was foreign to her there. Mother's peaks seemed higher, her lowlands bleaker, her chills colder, her beasts fiercer, her estrangement harsher. That was not why Daemiana slowed to a stop. Lights had become discernible in the faraway below. A coast, a town, that meant help. But it also warned of more males. One ended her life as she knew it—the ones after nearly killed her. Dionisio would surely if he ever found her. His capriccio had long skewed him, minting him the aficionado of everything wrong.

An arctic gust jarred her. Wilting conifers swayed and pelted her with their icy needles. Their aromatic beauty soothed her; their angst implored her to move on. All would soon be fine, she sang to them. Death over abomination, Daemiana reaffirmed and continued her descent. Hope was all she had left.

Night succumbed to dawn long before the toe of the mountain revealed itself to be a tangle of snowy brush, dense trees, and jagged boulders, all of which Daemiana wandered around and over with ease. None of it brought her any closer to the town, it seemed. It had looked so much nearer. A journey still laid ahead. That did not defer the unease. It was so vexing. Would the townspeople know? Would they stare? Would they judge? Would they attempt to harm her? Or would she find a way to meld? She felt no hurry to arrive, as badly as she needed the cover.

Daemiana was again skipping and caressing the trees she passed, taking her sweet time. Fear still wrung her heart, though it numbed to all else long ago. A mark of her accurst fix. No matter the outcome, the alternative was worse. She would be no male's prisoner any lon ger. That solemn vow began her journey and was something to be celebrated. So Daemiana pranced along for a great while. The end, whatever it was, beckoned—

She stopped and dove behind a boulder , clutching her mouth to muffle her terrified gasp. She looked around. Perhaps she had not smelled him sooner because he was downwind. Or was it a remnant odor? It took an apex predator to know one. Daemiana waited, listened. Unlike males, prudence was not something to which she was averse.

All was exquisitely silent. Daemiana resumed breathing. Her gaze slowly drifted upward to a passing flock. Those lithely pale soarers refused to be anything but free, like her. They were aficionados for all that was right. Oh, how every one of Mother's faces awed. Nothing more so than the green aurora glow which often haunted the night skies of this strange land, as it did her beloved Siberia. A lovely peculiarity was the only lingering familiarity.

Daemiana's eyes glistened. Could not Mother come to one day forgive her and show her mercy instead of wrath? Oh, how Daemiana longed to reconcile.

The birds dwindled to mere specks in the glowing horizon and were gone. Daemiana sighed. Her woe waded in drab silence. It was a silence all too silent. A silence that was not the least bit tranquil. It was an anomalous silence.

"No," Daemiana gasped before she could stop herself. "How did you find me?"

He had to be close, stalking her, yet perfectly still.

She felt compelled to reason with him.

"I wish you no ill, brother beast."

His silence mocked her.

"I desire only to be friends," she tried to console the vilely beast.

He was inconsolable. His silence rejected all cajoling.

"We are both children in Mother," Daemiana pleaded as she stood and backed away. "Unlike those who will ultimately come."

She tripped, stumbled, and fell. Daemiana stood and resumed backing away.

"Their presence alone will wilt your heart. They know no mercy."

She readied to flee the way she came — back up the mountain.

"Please let me pass, brother beast," Daemiana begged. "It is not too late for either of us."

She was unable to see him, yet certain he was there. She glanced in the direction of town, determined to reach it.

"I am your friend, and you are mine," she reassured the vilely beast, then plunged back into her journey toward the small coastal town, full sprint. She could not go back the way she came.

Daemiana scrambled to a stop as he emerged from the trees ahead. A heinous scar diagonally striated his face. Drool was oozing from his grotesquely disfigured snout. The fur on his hump was fully raised.

"L'assassino!" Daemiana chided him, accepting he would never forgive her for what she did to his face nights ago when she was not herself. "Wicked beast! It was you who drew first blood, not I!"

Her only regret had been failing to kill him—

The massive, scar-faced grizzly charged.

She fled the way she came. How did he get ahead of her? He and his brethren stood between her and her final hope — the small coastal town. It was then, Daemiana again reaffirmed what she had known all along but had resisted. She would have to be like every male she had ever known. Ruthless. For credence alone was the rhythm of life. It was the melody of self. It was the cadence of survival, and nothing else mattered.

CHAPTER 2

REGRETS ACHED MORE THAN WORN INNARDS AND AGED BONE. WORSE than those old breaks on the tundra and taiga grate. After decades alone in the gray, on the hunt, joy deferred, dreams forsaken; all for a greater good, at a better place, in another life. It made sense once. That had long waned by that year of our Lord, 1974.

Those spasms of doubt were cut short by a gnashing cough which yanked him back into the moment and task at hand, just breathing. He keeled over in the snow, gagging, frothing red onto the powdery, wintry canvas. His body seized till the fray let up. Nights were worse.

Ivers staggered back to his feet, small spade in hand. He resumed digging. With every thrust into the icy muck, his gashed face winced, and his mauled hands purpled. The long, rugged, brown coat on him dangled in shreds, intact only because of its metallic inner lining.

Strewn about were the tattered remnants of other armored coats, among the rhubarb bodies lying around, torn apart.

Rocks coddled fresh graves. They were in a better place. Ivers feebly hid the burials beneath brush, as best he could, wheezing and faltering until he collapsed against a nearby tree. He stared blankly into the nothingness, trembling, trying to catch his breath, clutching himself beneath the arms to warm his marred hands. Where did he go wrong? When? How did it all get there? The years had long become wailing ghosts. Gone, yet mourning what could have been. A life with Isabella. A something special that would have been cozy, hot, sacred, and messy. It would have worked. That became clear in retrospect. It had been a chance at a real life, a lifetime ago, if only he had sought love as fervently as his obsession with silencing macabre howls that tore through remote Siberian nights like butchering winds, spattering bloodied gobs and shards of prey. Alaska had not been kinder. It echoed that greatest regret.

Ivers hobbled to a mound in the snow, fell to his knees, and dug out his gear with the spade. The flurries had laid siege to it overnight. He strapped the spade to his rucksack and gingerly flung it onto his back by the shoulder straps, wincing in agony. Ivers then grabbed his rifle and writhed to his feet, and stumbled away. Jutting over his shoulder like a bloodied scorpion talon, from the sheath affixed to the back of his coat, was a sword handle. Whatever it was Ivers had survived; he had given as good as he got.

Dusk loomed as he meandered the remote wild, coughing violently. He lumbered past frostbitten boulders and trees, arriving eventually at a frozen river

He barely crawled across the thin, crackling ice on his stomach as it was breaking apart and beginning to drift away. Ivers made it onto terra firma before fully sinking, soaked, and shivering violently. He fixed his sights upstream, at something awaiting him in the distance, also on the riverbank. It was a small river cabin on stilts.

He stumbled along, inching closer and closer, stalked by the approaching night. A gallows crossbeam gradually became discernible beside the cabin. Busted chains dangled eerily from it, jingling in the breeze like some boding merriment. Beneath the gallows was a deep, underlying pit.

Ivers lurched for the cabin door, wheezing and shivering uncontrollably. He careened in, slammed the door shut, and dropped his gear as he fell to his knees. He struggled to light the logs in the woodstove.

Lackadaisical flames bobbled feebly. Ivers labored to swallow pills between coughing fits. He opened a jar, scooped his fingers in, and lathered the pungent, menthol rub all over his chest and throat.

He hunkered the pneumonia's onslaught in a sleeping bag on the cold floor. Amid fevered sweats and racking chills, billowy memories of Isabella's sensuous hands soothed him. She could caress away any misery. Illness had nothing on the torment of having chosen the wrong life, over her, decades ago, on faith alone. She had long become an angel of doubt, warning against a life unlived, in pursuit of fallacy. He couldn't die like this without making things right. That had been his ulterior motive, this final mission. But the engine of redemption was running on empty, and the fumes of dogma had long run out. A lesser man would have succumbed sooner.

The burdens of consciousness lifted for a precious few days.

"...the wisdom of the flesh is death."

Ivers slowly awoke.

"But the wisdom of the spirit is life and peace," Beaudry preached.

Two foreboding figures stood over Ivers, blocking the light radiating from the open door. It was day, and his last two remaining men, not the other side beckoning.

"We know where it escaped, brother," McConnolly reported. "A coastal mountain range."

Ivers sat up and rubbed his eyes. The illness was subsiding. He'd been given another chance at redemption.

"Where are—"

"Dead," Ivers rasped numbly, offering no explanation for his other mens' demise. None was needed.

The restrained fury in Beaudry's and McConnolly's eyes made it clear they understood. The others had been killed in action.

"We will persevere till we are as well. Or till this is finished," Ivers ordered.

Beaudry and McConnolly glanced subtly at one another.

"Ya deathly ill, brother," McConnolly tried to reason.

"Track it. Find it. Split up to cover more ground."

Only the most elite members of the Order survived a mission. Those who survived multiple missions were allowed to hunt alone, as Ivers had before age had confined him to again lead a team. Given the circumstance, they'd have to go on without him. So Ivers waved them off, frailly. He had never been more accepting of his imminent retirement from the Order altogether, even after decades alone in the gray.

"I won't be far," Ivers assured them, unwilling to slow them down. It was an age-old, black operation. "We are here to save souls. That is the mission."

CHAPTER 3

"AHHHHHHHHHHHHHHHHHHHHHH—"

The belay arrested his fall violently. It knocked the wind out of him hard and hurt worse than last time. He flailed and grasped at the mountain for mercy.

"Again," a voice casually said overhead.

"A-A-Again..." he stammered as he dangled 2,500 feet in the air, not okay. "O-O-Okay."

"Believe it."

Something wasn't right, not that he knew anything about it.

"I b-b-believe..." he conceded and reached for the friendliest rock on that convexly protruding section of the mountain, again. He stretched with all his might and finally grasped it. His muscles burned. The sweat was stinging his eyes. His spent fingers resumed twitching.

"I-I-I..."

"Do it. Believe it."

Nausea was setting in.

"Believe, and it'll be so."

"I b-b-believe."

Agony gnawed his every fiber. He tightened his grip on the rock, yanked himself flush against the mountain face, and shakily planted his tiptoes in a crevice. He curled himself slightly, took a deep breath, and thrusted himself upward, and grabbed another jagged edge. He tried to climb past the convex hump again.

"AHHHHHHHHHHHHHHHHHHHHH—"

The line arrested his fall so violently that his spine crackled. He couldn't breathe while dangling over what felt like the edge of the Earth.

"N-N-Need to go back down," he gasped, trying to catch his breath.

"Again."

"D-D-Dad—"

"There's more to life than just books n' theory. Believe it, Caelin."

Breath was still evading him. How was he going to get out of this alive?

"Don't be soft. You gotta do, you gotta be strong; that's what be'in a man's all about."

Caelin could only concede a weak nod.

"Mean it."

"O-O-Okay."

"Believe it."

"I...b-b-believe..."

"Now do it."

Stephen coolly watched Caelin from high above, climbing lead. Caelin avoided looking up at him, torn between the fear of dying and disappointing his father. But Caelin was already a stuttering, weakling of a disappointment. Nothing would ever change that.

Caelin extended his arms and body as far as he could while hanging from the line and began it all over again.

"That's it. Nice n' calm. Say it," Stephen mentored.

"C-C-Calm."

"Again."

"C-Calm."

"Again."

"Calm."

Same result.

"AHHHHHHHHHHHHHHHHHHH—"

The line arrested his fall more violently than ever. Caelin puked.

Above, Stephen stared up at the summit.

"Uh-huh."

Caelin descended the mountain a failure again, unable to even reach the snow line that time. He kept his eyes fixed on the ground.

Stephen flung the rest of his gear and rifle onto his back. Caelin held his breath as Stephen embarked back down the toe of the mountain and into the bush. Caelin did the same.

"Summit's not go'in anywhere. We'll bag it next time."

Caelin sighed with dread. Next time.

He moped along, lagging further and further behind. He couldn't see his father up ahead anymore. It was easy to lose someone in the bush. Maybe it was a good thing. Maybe that's what Dad wanted, to *lose* his loser son, all pathetic, eighteen stammering years of him. Maybe the mountain had been the last straw. Dad never treated him like a loser. Only pushed him to be strong. But Caelin wasn't. He knew it. Everyone did. Dad's denial couldn't go on forever. Caelin had to make things right before Dad gave up on him and began to see him the way everyone else did: like some chicken shit loser—

A twig snapped behind him.

Caelin flinched and spun around, glimpsing someone step behind a tree.

"Return the way you came," a female voice warned.

Caelin was petrified with fright.

"The beasts want blood."

Caelin was no closer to finding the words to respond.

Daemiana cautiously stepped out into the open, enshrouded head-to-toe in her hooded, crimson cloak. He glimpsed her bare feet as she neared, even more at a loss by it all. She seemed just as bewildered by his silence.

"They will kill you."

Caelin was too busy discerning her nude body through the slight opening in her cloak.

Daemiana's gaze went from curious to pensive to calculating. She drew closer and closer and closer.

Caelin's eyes widened as the red-cloaked specteress with an Italian accent leaned in and gently licked his lips.

"Save me," she hauntingly whispered.

He noticed ghastly bites on her body. He screamed, causing her to instinctually scratch his face as both fell back in horror of one another. They fled in opposite directions.

Caelin sprinted after his father, tripping over himself again and again until pathetically hitting the ground face-first, not far from the toe of his father's boot.

"I s-s-saw something—"

"No excuse for not staying calm. EVER."

Dad looked so appalled; he seemed not to want to even look at him. He merely glared straight ahead.

Caelin stared at the ground. Again, he had failed.

"Say it."

It was how Dad worked with him on his speech impediment.

"I-I-I'm calm."

"Again. Nice n' calm. Believe it."

"I-I'm calm."

"Again."

"I'm calm," he finally got out without a stutter.

The silence was tense.

"I know I've struggled to show it, but... I love you, son."

Caelin looked up at his father, mouth agape, not used to hearing niceties from him. He sensed something very wrong. Stephen was clutching his rifle, readying to use it.

"Close your eyes," Stephen ordered as he unclicked the safety. "Be calm."

Caelin gasped. Had Dad finally lost it? Was he gonna finally off his loser son, put him down like some lame animal? Like those tales about Dad's temper when he was younger; how he almost killed some guy for spilling his beer or something.

"I-I-I'm gonna be tougher. I swear," Caelin pleaded. "I-I-I'll turn it around—"

"It's all my fault, the way things turned out. My failures as a man."

"I'm volunteering a-a-at the clinic and the chapel—"

"I took you in after your mama passed, not cause I had to."

"I'm devoting m-m-my life to helping others—"

"But cause I finally stopped running from my obligations."

"I swear."

"My obligations as a man, as a father, who walked out on you and your mother."

"D-D-Dad—"

"I pushed you hard cause didn't want you to wind up a coward."

Caelin sobbed for his life.

"A coward like me, son. Who stopped believing and panicked in the face of doing what was right."

"I swear..."

"Always stay calm, now more than ever. Believe it."

"Wh-Wh-Why are you saying all this?"

"Cause the nearest climbable tree's 50 feet away. Behind me. Calmly walk to it. Climb it. Now, WALK."

Caelin finally realized that Stephen wasn't aiming the rifle at him but instead past him, at a massive, charging grizzly.

Stephen fired off one, two, three shots.

Caelin's ears rung as the monstrous bear crashed down to the ground, inches from him — dead. He stared at its enormous head in shock. What...?

"WALK!"

Caelin was jolted by his father's words and jumped to his feet. He finally saw what his father had known all along. Beyond the surrounding brush, there were massive, anomalous grizzlies, each foaming at the mouth with fury. Caelin ran for the tree in panic.

"No! WALK!"

Two bears charged after him.

Stephen took aim.

Caelin cowered as the first bear closed in on him but was struck by three rifle blasts and fell at Caelin's feet, thrashing around.

The other bear pounced on Caelin. Before it could maul him, that bear too was shot once, twice, and finally a third time. It keeled over on top of Caelin.

Caelin crawled out from beneath the dying bear and resumed his hysterical sprint toward the tree.

Stephen again reloaded and readied to defend himself against the bears moving in on him as—

Caelin reached the tree and began climbing. He lost his shaky footing and fell. A bear pounced on him and began mauling him. Caelin was sprayed with warm blood as it also was struck by three rifle blasts.

Two bears pounced on Stephen before he could shoot them. He skillfully fought them off using his ice axe and broke free. But—

The biggest, most horrific bear — the beast with the disfigured snout and the diagonal, claw scar across its face — stood on its hind legs behind Stephen, towering eleven feet.

Caelin screamed as the scar-faced bear crashed down on Stephen and tore into the back of his head. It then thrashed him around like a rag doll.

With stunning speed, Daemiana ran up and smacked the bear on the head.

"Release him, wicked beast!"

The bears grew more enraged at the sight of her. The fur on their backs raised. They charged after her. She fled with the bears in hot pursuit.

Caelin stumbled to his gravely injured Dad and knelt beside him.

"Dad..."

"You're okay..."

"I'm s-s-sorry. Sorry I couldn't climb the tree."

"You...did fine..."

"Sorry, I c-c-couldn't help..." Caelin sobbed.

Stephen's scalp was torn off.

He grabbed Caelin's hand.

The pool of blood beneath them grew bigger and bigger.

"I'm sorry, Dad—"

"Nevermind... Just believe... Always believe... And..."

Stephen convulsed and slipped away.

CHAPTER 4

THE PREDAWN BITE DIPPED BELOW FREEZING. HE FELL DEEPER INTO the throes of shock and hypothermia. He was sitting beside his dead father, rocking, mumbling, shivering.

"Summit's n-n-not go'in anywhere. We'll bag it n-n-next time. N-N-Next time..."

Something was traversing the bush. It slowed to a stop. The figure drew nearer and nearer until it stood over Caelin and his father's corpse. It was a huntsman clutching a rifle.

"No..." he sighed. "Caelin?"

Caelin finally looked up at the huntsman, who many called Hermit Lawson.

Evening loomed. Caelin was being lugged along, barely conscious; his feet were dragging across the ground, his arm over Hermit Lawson's shoulders.

They eventually emerged from the open wild and descended into the outskirts of a tiny coastal town. The decrepit chapel at town's edge awaited like a sentinel, both guarding and overlooking its borough. They collapsed at its steps.

Caelin stared numbly at the ground. He was sitting on the chapel steps with a musty blanket draped over his shoulders while Lawson spoke to the town sheriff and chapel priest.

Dad couldn't be dead. He was too strong, too tough. He climbed all the highest peaks in the world. He bagged every big game animal from Africa to the Arctic. He sailed around the world, solo. He lived in Alaska cause he refused to live a dull, conventional, chicken shit life. He refused to accept weakness. Maybe, it's why Dad left when Caelin was only two. Maybe he sensed a loser son and refused to be dragged down. And that's just what ended up happening, wasn't it? He'd been dragged down. Caelin choked back a sob and wiped away snot and tears. He watched Lawson describe what he saw to Sheriff Dollins and Father Wallace. They were all old friends of Dad. Would they blame Caelin for what happened?

"Whereabouts?" Sheriff Dollins asked Lawson.

"Body's 'bout half a day's trek, northeast. Give or take, if ya move fast."

"I'll bring him home, then organize a hunt for the grizzly."

"Grizzlies, Sheriff. Several by the looks of it."

"Grizzlies are solitary," Sheriff Dollins replied.

"Not these, I guess. I gotta get goin'. If I see'em, I'll take'em out," Lawson said as he cocked his rifle.

"Careful out there. Don't let'em take *you* out."

Lawson scoffed as Father Wallace rubbed his brow with grief.

"Hell knows better than to come a call'in me, Sheriff, ya know that. I'll take it over—"

"Sensitivity will be imperative," Father Wallace snapped. "Caelin lost his mother not long ago. Now this, my God."

"He was my friend too, Father, n' he liked my jokes."

Other townsmen were assembling rifles and flashlights in hand. The news had spread. Caelin fixed his sights on the ground again as Hermit Lawson approached, placed a hand on his shoulder.

"If there's anything ya need, ya know where to find me."

Caelin watched Lawson embark back into the wild and begin his long trek back home to a remote hunting shack.

A tall, foreboding man in a long, brown, hooded coat was suddenly there, glaring down at Caelin. It was McConnolly.

"Why aren't ya telling the truth, brother?"

His Irish accent bewildered Caelin as much as the question.

"W-W-What?"

"About what happened out there."

"I..."

"Stranger things have happened, I suppose. Then with time, a rational explanation ensues, n' it turns out the happening wasn't strange at all. It was inevitable."

"Uh…"

"Disturbed n' encroached ecosystems sometimes cause animals to snap n' attack humans. Nice, yeah? Payback."

"I don't kn-kn-know—"

"Except bears don't much travel in packs, hunting people. Ever. Even as their habitats were decimated and they were extirpated from three-quarters of North America. Ya know, they once roamed freely as apex predators, from Mexico to Alaska. Now, all of a sudden, this? Why don't ya tell me what really happened out there?"

"I told the truth—"

"Caelin, is it?"

"Uh—"

"Sure, what attacked ya out there…was indeed bears?"

Caelin stared at McConnolly, at a loss for words, and instead glimpsing a huge, chrome dagger strapped to his chest through a small opening in his coat.

Father Wallace approached and patted Caelin on the back sympathetically.

"How are you holding up, son?"

Father Wallace stared at McConnolly.

"I don't believe we've met. You are...?"

"A friend, Father," McConnolly replied with a warm smile and strolled away. "Just here to help."

"How so, sir? What brings you to Kreuger Sound?"

They watched McConnolly slip back into the night as eerily as he appeared.

CHAPTER 5

Sparse fog crept in from the eerily still Pacific. Bleak wilderness fronting icy peaks abutted the small town on all other ends. Its rotting signboard dangled by rusty hinges on a weary post, cawing weakly in the breeze like an ailing crow. It read: KREUGER SOUND, ALASKA.

Ivers mulled every nuance of the place's drear. The old fishing town looked worse for the wear than him. He finally encountered something more scourged by the years. That gave him a morbid solace after narrowly surviving his last bout with death. It still lingered in his bones and soul.

He gazed out at the ocean to put it out of his mind. Seals were basking on a nearby iceberg. Terra firma was always safest. After decades assessing all angles in the remote Siberian wild, hunting the predator of all predators, looking for death in all directions, he knew a bad move when he saw one.

Ivers closed his eyes in hopes of shutting out thoughts of death and of where it could flank or descend from at any moment. If only for a second. He could not ease his guard enough to breathe in the serenity. It was merely the lull before the storm. His eyes grew misty as he tried to recall his last moment of peace. There would be no getting any closer than that. Whatever calm there was in him had long slid into the void. It was time to begin.

He searched every docked trawler. Empty. He scrutinized every rig, every building, everything he passed, and even every track and footprint on the dirt of the town's only road, from where it began at the docks to the old chapel at town's edge. Still, there was not a soul anywhere. Where had everyone gone? Where were Beaudry and McConnolly? They had surely arrived before him. Ivers again found himself standing before the lonely chapel at town's edge, as he had upon his arrival, out from the open wild.

He climbed the steps and opened the double doors this time. He entered silently and stood off to the side. The standing room was scarce. It was filled to capacity. The townsfolk were mourning the man in the casket. It was a funeral. That explained the deserted town.

Ivers quietly left the chapel and looked in every direction. He resumed scrutinizing every detail. The dead man had been a fisherman by trade, an avid outdoorsman for leisure. His adolescent son had only suffered minor injuries during the bear attack. A son who was nowhere to be seen and who wasn't at the service, it seemed.

Why would he not attend his own father's funeral? A father who a marauding horde of rogue bears had killed. Something improbable under normal circumstances. If Beaudry and McConnolly were on the right track, they'd be assessing the site of the bear attack after thoroughly having canvassed the town. That's where they were, Ivers deduced.

Now, where would a boy who hadn't attended his own father's funeral be? What exactly had happened out there? Ivers turned to face the chapel and watched the procession head toward the nearby graveyard with the casket. He went on ahead.

The drab, greenish hue of cold, dank, algal gloom adorned each tombstone. More so than the rest of the town. As Ivers neared, he discerned a haunting figure in the burial grounds, alone and glaring down at a freshly dug grave. It was a chilling sight even for Ivers' hardened eyes. Had the boy been there the entire time?

The townsfolk made their way out of the graveyard as the casket was buried. Ivers lingered, observing the boy, who was still in the same spot, motionless and stoic. It was as if he had not moved in hours. The parish priest and town sheriff remained by his side in silence. They occasionally exchanged solemn glances, appearing unsure what to say. The silence was then broken.

"I k-k-killed him..."

The poor kid had a stutter. Nothing about life was fair.

"What?" the Sheriff replied.

"Caelin, you did not kill your dad," the parish priest said.

"If I had only c-c-climbed the tree..."

"God called him home," the parish priest said. "That's all."

"We'll walk you home," soothed the Sheriff. "I'm gonna get the bears that did it. I promise you that. They're the only ones at fault here."

Ivers churned inside, all too familiar with that kind of guilt. But unlike the boy, he truly had blood on his hands. His missteps had invariably cost lives, including Isabella's. The boy had learned the hard way that if the cold or the terrain didn't get you, something with teeth would. For such was the nature of the Alaskan and Siberian wilderness—

A young woman was sprinting toward the graveyard. Ivers subtly slipped a hand beneath his coat and gripped his gun as he discerned her face. She was in medical garb. The young nurse was not the target.

"Daddy!" she yelled.

"Lori. What is it, darl'in?" the Sheriff replied.

"The girl you found is alive."

"What?"

"What girl?" asked the parish priest.

The Sheriff seemed unable to fathom it.

"What girl?" the priest asked again.

"Another victim of the bears, we think. The posse n' me found her the other day when out hunting for'em..." the Sheriff muttered, mostly to himself, while staring at his daughter with disbelief. "What exactly you say'in, sweetheart? Cause that can't be right."

The boy grew deathly pale.

A chill came over Ivers. He'd seen it, no doubt!

Ivers slipped away hurriedly, loathing himself for feeling his struggles with faith creeping back. It had made him soft, weak, derelict, unfit to continue. Faith was all one had in this line of work, but his was fading and time was fleeting. He was going to kill it this time, after breaking it. To make everything right.

CHAPTER 6

SHE HAD ROUSED TO AN ABERRANT BLACK, SCREAMED, AND FLAILED against some smothering cocoon. She tore through the imprisoning body bag and toppled off the metal gurney, and hit her head on the floor. The rank of stagnant death hit her harder than the pain. Daemiana leapt to her feet and stumbled through the darker than dark, knocking over another gurney and the corpse on it. She screamed again as she clawed at the imprisoning metal door until the last thing she remembered dawned on her. She ran her bloodied fingers over the macabre wounds to her body. Dizzied by the memory of the beasts mauling her apart, she leaned against the frigid wall, slid to the floor, and drifted back into the black.

She awakened on a balmy bed in a weighty cocoon of bandages, blankets, and tubes; her agonies were lulled. The soft light soothed her, if only for a moment. She had no idea how much time had gone by. Engaging the beasts had been foolish. The price of doing good was always too high. From morgue to the infirmary, was it not supposed to be the other way around? What would they think? She had just arrived in the small town, and already its haven and respite were fouled. Any males aware of what had happened already knew too much. They were at their worst when wielding all control.

Daemiana yanked off the tube, streaming air to her nose. She ripped out the needles seeping fluids into her veins. She climbed off the bed and noticed on herself a short, white gown. Daemiana tip-toed to the coat hanger on the wall, grabbed her ravaged cloak, and inched toward the open door.

She peeked into a dim corridor. No one. She snuck along, unsure where to go. Every room she passed was dark. They all looked alike. The floor was most unsettling. It resembled the one in the morgue — cold, smooth, drab white. She tried to put it out of her mind as she neared the end of the hall, where a small waiting area abutted the entrance to a well-lit office. The exit felt near—

"D-D-Doctor Schmidt!" an approaching male shouted.

She crept into the dark space beneath a wooden bench in the waiting area. A male rushed from the opposite way into the office.

"Doctor Schmidt!"

"Caelin. What is it, son?"

"I-I-Is it true?"

She awaited her chance to slip out of the infirmary unnoticed.

"I'm so sorry about your father, Caelin. Sorry I couldn't attend the service. I have a patient—"

"A g-g-girl...?"

"Son, you're pretty fragile right now. Go home."

Daemiana inched out, readying to rush past the office, no longer caring if she was seen. She dove back into the shadows as two other males arrived and rushed into the office.

"Sheriff Dollins. Father Wallace," Doctor Schmidt greeted them. "I trust you're here to walk young Caelin back home. There's really nothing to see here."

"Doc, that gal was dead."

"Sheriff. It was an honest mistake—"

"Mistake nothin', Doc. I know dead when I see it."

"Sometimes, the inexplicable happens," Father Wallace interjected.

"C'mon, Father, save the miracle talk for your sermons."

"You may want to listen to Father Wallace, Sheriff."

"Doc, all that aside. Only way in or out of town is by boat. We're surrounded by mountains on all other sides. So either that naked gal swam here or climbed over them damn peaks."

Daemiana inched forward again, having heard enough, ready to flee past them all. Again, she dove back into the shadows. A tall, menacing figure stealthily rushed by, unnoticed by the others. He silently stormed each patient room with one hand resting on his gun and his other hand resting on his dagger, both weapons discreetly holstered beneath his long coat. It was Ivers. That meant the other killers would not be far, or perhaps they were already outside lying in wait.

Crippled with fright, Daemiana was unsure whether to flee anymore. She peered past the office to the far end of the corridor. The young nurse exited a room and sat at the front desk. Daemiana feared for her life, too, for all their lives. The aficionado of death had arrived and was visiting them—

Ivers rushed back and stormed the office.

"Where is the patient?" Ivers rasped.

"Who the hell are you?" the Sheriff replied.

"You can't just barge in here—" Dr. Schmidt said.

"The patient is gone!" Ivers growled. "Where is she?"

"What?" Dr. Schmidt asked. "Impossible!"

"Not askin' you again. Identify yourself," the Sheriff demanded.

"A friend. Now find the patient!"

"I don't answer to you—"

"And evacuate the town!" Ivers warned.

"You're outta your mind—"

"Bears are not the problem, Sheriff. EVACUATE THE TOWN," Ivers ordered as he stormed out the way he came, past the perplexed nurse.

"Get back here!" Sheriff Dollins rushed after him.

Dr. Schmidt rushed the opposite way toward the patient rooms, followed by Father Wallace and Caelin.

Daemiana remained in hiding, still unsure whether or not to flee. The wilderness was her only escape. But the town was possibly her last hope. Perhaps, a local male could be persuaded to help her. Which one?

The doctor, the priest, and the boy searched each room again on their way back. The Sheriff returned.

"She was too gravely hurt to have run out of here, Sheriff!" Dr. Schmidt said. "Where's that man? He knows something!"

"Son of a bitch disappeared. I radioed it in. My boys'll find him," the Sheriff reassured.

Just then, the boy spotted her hiding place and locked eyes with her. Daemiana gasped.

"W-W-Wait…" he said, approaching slowly.

She closed her eyes and curled up like a possum to play dead. She had decided to stay rather than flee.

She was in a patient's bed again.

The local males were arguing in the hall outside.

"She's damn strong n' healthy for a gal who was dead when I found her, Doc," said the Sheriff.

"I'm done arguing medical mysteries with you," replied the doctor.

"Gentlemen. May we please focus on the task at hand?" suggested the priest. "Who is this girl? Where did she come from? Why is that man after her?"

Daemiana opened her eyes slowly, only to realize the boy was staring at her from the hall. She closed them again. He hesitated, approached, and stood at her bedside.

"I r-r-remember..." the boy said.

Daemiana ignored him.

"Y-Y-You tried to save us from the bears."

Silence.

"I'll stay. And protect you too," Caelin assured her.

Daemiana opened her eyes and sized him up. The boy was weak and harmless. He could not protect anyone, including himself. He had put up no fight against the beasts. She closed her eyes dismissively.

"Night is near. Flee, or you will die," she warned.

Caelin stepped back, shaken by the notion.

He jumped as Dr. Schmidt grabbed his shoulder and escorted him back into the hallway.

"Young man, you have no business in there. She needs her rest, as do you. You just lost your father."

"Just w-w-wanna help—"

"Doctor Schmidt is right, Caelin. Go home. We will figure this out," Father Wallace advised. "If you really want to help, please return to the chapel and close it for the night."

"But I volunteer h-h-here too—"

"As a favor to me," Father Wallace insisted.

Daemiana slowly opened her eyes again and fixed them on the boy as he nodded. On second thought, out of all of them, the boy seemed the most *helpful.*

CHAPTER 7

The afternoon faded into early evening. Caelin bolted out from the clinic and embarked on the short trek to the lonely chapel at town's edge.

"Hey, Caelin. Wait up," shouted the young nurse at the front desk, the lovely Lori. She rushed out after him.

Caelin slowed to a stop and turned. Shit. He struggled to make eye contact with her, as always.

"I just wanted to say..."

He resented her sympathies. He resented them long before his father's death. He'd loved her ever since he could remember. All she could ever muster in return was pity for the stuttering village idiot. Disdain had always been easier to swallow than her brand of kindness.

"Yeah, w-w-well... It happens."

Her pained expression informed him that it was the worst possible thing he could have said. Their interactions were always dismally awkward.

"I just wanted to say how sorry I am. We all loved your father."

Caelin nodded and continued on his way. Lori Dollins — Sheriff Dollins' daughter — was only two years older than him, but they might as well have been decades and miles apart.

"If there's anything I can do," she went on sympathetically.

No, there wasn't; he waved politely as he went. He was just the stammering fool who came to live with Dad after Mom died, and she was the village princess. Beautiful, charitable, sweet, and whose boyfriend was the biggest asshole in town. The guy would mock Caelin's stutter sometimes.

"Anything, okay?" she persisted.

Fuck, already. Her pity stung worse than indifference. It reminded him that he was just some stray dog to her, rather than the knight in shining armor he yearned to be.

"You know what, hold on. My shift is over. Daddy and I'll walk you."

Caelin spun around pleadingly.

"N-N-No, I'm good, Lori—"

"With those rogue bears out there, we can't be too safe. Hold on."

Caelin moped along, wanting to be anywhere but with Lori and Sheriff Dollins strolling alongside, coddling him. He tuned them out. His eyes drifted to the furthest peak in the distance — the one he and Dad had attempted that day. Lori's presence was filling Caelin with memories of him. As with everything else, Stephen had pushed Caelin hard to go for it and act on his feelings for Lori. Who cared if she had a boyfriend? And like with everything else, Caelin balked. Altogether, the pressures Dad had put on him were unbearable. For a moment, Caelin's eyes watered with relief that he was dead—

"Ain't that right?" the Sheriff asked. "Caelin?"

"Uh, y-y-yeah," Caelin replied, to whatever it was they were talking about.

"Really, you think she's pretty?" Lori said with a big, perplexed smile.

"Who?" Caelin asked.

"Our patient. The girl!"

"Oh."

"Our very own sleep'in beauty," the Sheriff jibed as he patted Caelin on the back. "Maybe you can ask her out once she's all better."

"Eww. Come on, Dad. She's creepy. Where did she come from?"

"Dunno, darl'in. But I'll figure it out once I get back n' question her."

"Whatever. Okay, we're here."

They had arrived at the homes across from the Sheriff's Office and its adjacent kennel-barn, where the search-and-rescue horses and hounds were housed.

"Come in for some supper before you go," Lori told Caelin.

"N-N-Not hungry. Thank you."

"C'mon, you gotta eat," advised the Sheriff.

Caelin shook his head. Lori hugged him and entered the home. Sheriff Dollins lingered pensively. There was a long silence.

"You know, I lost my old man when I was not much older than you."

Caelin looked down.

"Well, just wanna say, you're hold'in up better than I did."

Caelin nodded solemnly, unsure whether reality had fully sunk in yet.

"Your daddy was a good man. And a good friend. But he was wrong."

Caelin looked up, surprised. Wrong?

"Stephen was too hard on you if you ask me. I figure he was just overcompensat'in up for miss'in the first sixteen years of your life."

Sixteen sounded about right, give or take. Caelin never bothered with the math; it was too painful. Caelin looked down again, not sure what the Sheriff was getting at.

"I guess I'm say'in; he was wrong to think that you were too soft just because you were book-smart and preferred the indoors."

"I l-l-let him down."

"He was only be'in the Dad he knew how to be. Spend'in time with you, teaching ya climb'in, hunt'in, horseback, survival."

"I wasn't good a-a-at any of it."

"Don't sell yourself short. It's stuff that took him a lifetime to master. It made him happy. He was just pass'in on to you. Father to son."

Caelin nodded again, too numb to understand.

"Almost forgot," Sheriff Dollins said as he pulled something from his pocket. "I recovered this off the ground when I brought your daddy home."

Sheriff Dollins handed Caelin a cross pendant. Stephen's cross pendant. Caelin stared at it, number than ever.

"I don't w-w-want it. It should've been buried w-w-with him."

"Caelin, I'm giv'in it to you because I don't think it should've been buried with him. You need something of your Dad to hold on to."

"I can't," Caelin said and handed it back.

"Stephen was a man of strong, quiet faith. He didn't wear it on his sleeve, but he believed."

Caelin was jolted violently by the idea.

The Sheriff put the pendant back in Caelin's hand. Caelin felt a smoldering rage bubbling up to the surface.

"Why did he hate m-m-me, then? And treat me like shit?!" Caelin exploded. "Why?! If he *believed*?"

"Caelin."

And with that, Caelin stormed off alone to the chapel at town's edge.

CHAPTER 8

IT WAS ABOUT A THREE-QUARTER MOON ADORNING THE GREENISH AU-rora twilight. The open wild was eyeing the old chapel at town's edge like prey. Caelin was on the steps, glaring at his father's pendant. The guy nailed to it had too much faith for his own good. What was the point? Bad shit happened no matter what, and there was no making it right. So, Caelin had to just lock up the damn chapel like he'd been asked and quit dwelling on it all.

He stood and approached the double doors, keys in hand.

"Close'in up a wee bit early, don't ya think, brother?"

Caelin flinched, dropped the keys, and cowered as he looked back. McConnolly was emerging from the bush in full gear, with a sword strapped to his back. A dagger was strapped to his chest diagonally, and guns were strapped to his hips, visible only because his long coat was open.

"Didn't mean to scare ya."

Caelin labored not to run away. Weaponry aside, there was a lurking, violent intensity to the guy not brimming in regular people. He was a killer.

"The chapel closes at n-n-n-night."

"Always lock up without check'in if anyone's inside?"

The question irked Caelin as much as the nosy, condescending tone.

"N-N-None of your business," Caelin blurted before he could stop himself.

McConnolly leaped over the steps and got in Caelin's face, making him flinch again. The guy seemed even taller up close. Caelin looked down and regretted his surge of defiance. He never stood up for himself. Why had he chosen to start with this psycho?

"So you're the groundskeeper?"

The sight of the dagger and guns beneath McConnolly's long, thick, brown coat made Caelin shiver. The coat's insides seemed to be lined with chain mail armor.

"I just v-v-volunteer—"

"I heard ya didn't even enter the chapel for ya dad's funeral."

Caelin kept his mouth shut and eyes down. He didn't have to explain himself to this weird, Irish fucker—

"Three reasons why someone won't set foot in a church. One, he's possessed. Two, he's of a different belief. Or three, *he's angry at God.*"

Caelin was overcome by a surge of anger. He looked McConnolly straight in the eye.

"Fuck you."

McConnolly smiled warmly.

"Ya finally stood up for yourself and meant it, brother. Good for you. Keep it up."

Patronizing dick. He didn't seem much older. Maybe it was why all his crap stung so much. Caelin had been bullied his whole life by smug assholes like him. Now, in front of a chapel too. It had to stop, one way or another—

"I cordially request that ya not close the chapel, brother. My associates are inside. Pray'in."

"Can y-y-you make them leave?"

McConnolly instead turned and stared into the open wild.

"Ya, know. I went out to where it happened. And saw all the bear tracks. I believe ya now. Bears did it; they killed ya Dad. But your tracks seem to place ya with someone barefoot. Before the attack, I presume."

Caelin's heart sank.

McConnolly turned and looked him straight in the eye.

"Seen her since?" he grinned.

Caelin just stared back.

"It's imperative ya tell the truth, brother. You'll be saving lives. Includ'in your own."

Caelin looked down again, his mind racing. Did he want to hurt her? Did the other guy at the clinic want to hurt her too? Caelin slowly shook his head: no.

McConnolly's expression became sympathetic.

"Find solace in that the bears were only after her, not you n' your Dad. You were just at the wrong place at the wrong time. I'm sorry."

The grief hit Caelin's throat hard, making his eyes water. It took every ounce of strength in him not to sob—

Caelin flinched as the chapel's double doors swung open. Two tall, foreboding men stormed out, also in long coats and full gear. One of them was the psycho from the clinic. The other pressed a dagger against Caelin's face. He was the most menacing of the three. His icy blue eyes never blinked.

"Behold, he that is unbelieving, his soul shall not be right in himself: but the just shall live in his faith."

Caelin felt warmth streaming down his leg.

"Beaudry," Ivers barked, clearly the leader. "McConnolly. Let's go."

Beaudry removed the dagger from Caelin's face.

"No stone unturned," Ivers ordered.

They raised their hoods over their heads and stormed into the night in different directions. All three wore identical, long, rugged, hooded, brown coats.

Caelin remained where he stood, still in shock, clutching the dagger imprint on his face. The warmth of his pissed pants dissipated and was becoming cold and clammy. He resumed breathing. Caelin choked back a relieved sob. He had to alert Sheriff Dollins so he could protect the girl from them!

CHAPTER 9

Caelin rushed into the adjacent rectory and slammed the door shut behind him. He crawled through the dark, fumbled around, and knocked over a chair and a lamp. The shards cut into his knees as he grabbed the phone. He struggled to dial in the dark, wincing in pain.

The phone at the other end of the line rang and rang.

Caelin hung up, dialed another number.

"Hello."

"L-L-Lori..."

"Caelin?"

"I n-n-need the Sheriff."

"Daddy had supper and went back to the clinic to question the patient. You okay?"

"I called the clinic. N-N-No answer."

"Well, they're busy, Caelin. Trying to help the girl."

"But... I..."

"What's the matter?"

"S-S-Something happened..."

"What?"

"I'll...call the clinic a-a-again—"

"Caelin, you're not well. Go to sleep—"

Caelin hung up, irked. Even panicked, he hated that dismissive pity. He dialed again and crept around in the dark. Caelin glanced out the window as the clinic phone rang and rang. Were those three psychos still out there? Would they come back to kill him?

He sat in a dark corner on the floor, letting the phone at the other end of the line ring on and on and on. Someone had to answer eventually.

"Hello. Hello?"

Caelin jumped. Someone had finally answered.

"Who is this?" said the voice at the other end of the line.

Caelin pulled focus. Hours had passed. It looked like dawn outside.

"Hello!"

Caelin grabbed the phone off the floor, realizing he must have dozed off, remembering and regretting he'd been too chickenshit to leave the rectory.

"H-H-Hello, Sheriff Dollins?!" Caelin yelled into the phone.

"No. Who's this?"

"I n-n-need the Sheriff!"

There was a tense silence.

"Hello?"

"Caelin, that you? This is Deputy Bob."

"Deputy Bob? Y-Y-You're at the clinic too?"

There was another tense silence. What was going on?

"I was attacked last night," Caelin finally blurted.

"You survived the clinic attack?" Deputy Bob said ominously.

"Uh... No. Wh-Wh-What?"

"Stay indoors. Must've been the same bear."

"What bear?"

That was the longest, tensest silence yet.

"Wh-Wh-What happened?!" Caelin asked as his heart sank. "I wanna talk to the Sheriff or Father W-W-Wallace!"

"Stay put," Deputy Bob ordered.

"I-I-I'm coming over—"

"Not until we kill this bear!"

Caelin jumped to his feet. What fucking bear?!

"Put on the Sheriff, Father W-W-Wallace, or Dr. Schmidt!" Caelin demanded.

"Listen to me—"

"I'm coming o-o-over—"

"No!" Deputy Bob shouted, then sighed with reluctance. "They're dead, Caelin—"

Caelin dropped the phone and bolted for the door. He sprinted out of the rectory and back toward the center of town, where the clinic was. The three psychos had killed them to get to the girl!

Red caught the corner of his eye in the drab of the neighboring woods. Caelin stopped and stared, then resumed running, but again stopped. He could discern her long, burgundy locks anywhere. He drew nearer, past the brush. He knew for sure it was her, laying beneath her crimson cloak. She seemed to be breathing. She had survived the attack.

As he lifted her up into his arms, he realized she was nude beneath the crimson of her hooded cloak. The more he resisted a second glance, if only to be sure, the more he fixated on it while carrying her back to the rectory. He hated himself for it, given everything that had happened. Was she some kind of moral or karmic test? Is that why he found her near the chapel? Not that he believed in God or hell or anything like that. But what was going through his mind wasn't right.

She seemed about the same age as him, maybe a bit older. Where was she from? The nearest other town was hundreds of miles away, by sea. Endless nothing awaited over the mountainous wilderness and snowcapped peaks that abutted Kreuger Sound on all other sides. How did she arrive? Why?

He set her down too quickly and winced as her head bumped the wooden floor of the rectory. He stared at her anxiously. Before he knew it, he had to stop himself from admiring the sleek, ambrosial curvatures of her face. His heart raced, and his belly sank. Something about her rasped him with strange unease; a savage unknown tangled with sweet familiarity; a something menacing yet violently longed. Lori was beautiful, but this girl was something else.

He noticed her cloak was covered with dry blood. He drew closer and parted it slowly, only to notice that her body was too. He looked for a wound. There was none. Wasn't the blood hers? Had her wounds all healed? What the...

Before he could mull over his confusion, he glimpsed her nude breast. His lips quivered. He was unable to look away, only to realize she was awake and glaring at him pensively. He stumbled back, mortified. He was a fucking pervert.

"I'm sorry—"

Caelin flinched as Daemiana pounced on him like a predator on prey, knocking him onto his back and straddling him, never once breaking her stare. She licked, kissed, and nibbled his lips as if starved for a man. Caelin sat up and pushed her back despite the hypnotic beauty of her emerald eyes, burgundy hair, and perfect skin and figure.

"What h-h-happened at the clinic?" he asked, at a loss for breath.

Daemiana just stared at him as if not knowing what he was talking about. Caelin stood and grabbed the phone. She jumped to her feet and hugged him tightly, lovingly, as if starved for warmth and intimacy too. Her sagebrush-like scent and caressing softness made him forget who he wanted to call. No one was more starved for it all than him. The dulcet sedation and intoxication of a woman's love was something he'd never known—

But people were dying out there because of those murderous psychos and rogue bears. What the hell was going on? Caelin had dialed with urgency, and the phone at the other end of the line was finally answered.

"Bishop," Caelin said. "I didn't kn-kn-know who else to call. It's me, Caelin, the groundskeeper a-a-at Kreuger Sound Parish—"

Daemiana was licking Caelin's ear, making him nearly forget what he was saying. He couldn't get himself to push away her affections again.

"Father Wallace is dead," Caelin continued.

Daemiana began love biting Caelin's throat.

"You both said to call y-y-you if there was ever an emergency..."

She kissed his mouth.

"Send help—" Caelin mumbled before tossing the phone.

Okay, what the fuck was going on? Not that he wanted her kisses to stop. He'd never been surer of anything else in his life. All the fear, nerves, angst, feelings of inadequacy, and weakness that hovered over him always, like a little black cloud, were suddenly gone, replaced with intoxicating exhilaration and confidence.

"Help me," she whispered.

"Yes," he replied boldly, again never surer of anything else as he feasted on her. He couldn't believe it was happening, with a girl like her. That was what it must have felt like to be a man. He never wanted it to end.

Caelin's hands glided down her body, but she gently nudged them away. Again, she love-bit him while slowly running her sharp nails down his chest. She then cowered and gasped. The cross pendant had fallen from his coat pocket and hit the floor.

"Are you one of them?"

"What...?" Caelin barely got out.

"Zealot. Monster. Inquisitor!"

Daemiana fled, horrified.

Caelin was too aroused to even realize what had happened. He tried to stumble after her in a sweaty daze, never having seen anyone run away so fast. He saw the pendant on the floor.

"It's not even mine!"

CHAPTER 10

Daemiana escaped the odious boy and fled into the open wild. The boy trusted in something other than Mother Nature. Religion was an indulgence as rotten as it was hollow, one she refused to ever again indulge. That boy was as pitiful as when she saved him from the beasts. He would not survive a single night with her—

A ferocious blow to the chest — to a loud, searing hiss — knocked her back as her momentum flung her legs forward. Her head hit the ground hard. She retched and gagged, nauseated by the taste of her own blood filling her mouth. Daemiana tried to sit up. A dagger was lodged in her heart. Oh, dearest Mother...

A male was emerging from the shadows.

Had he thrown it?

She tried to crawl away into the refuge of the bush. Was he Ivers? Or was he another secret, present-day Inquisitor?

"In repentance and rest is your salvation, in quietness and trust is your strength, but you would have none of it."

Oh no... It was the deadliest of them all, the one who spoke only in riddles.

Beaudry grabbed her hair and dragged her away, back toward the chapel.

He kicked open the chapel doors and dragged her in, past the pews, up onto the sanctuary floor, beside the altar. He yanked his dagger from her chest and melded into the shadows as—

The boy rushed the chapel entrance and stood at the doors, looking for her, appearing oblivious to what was happening, seemingly interested only in resuming their lusty havoc.

"Th-Th-The pendant's not mine," the boy called out to her. "Okay?"

Daemiana pleaded in tangled wails.

"It's just a cross," Caelin pleaded back while glaring at the cross on the alter, reluctant to enter, seemingly having his own differences with it and what it stood for.

But his attraction for her was stronger than his aversion to the chapel, so he rushed in. She was sloshing weakly in her ponding blood, trying to crawl away as it oozed down the sanctuary steps while Caelin drew closer and closer in dismay.

She flinched at the sight of Beaudry emerging behind him. Beaudry struck Caelin on the head with the butt of his dagger, knocking him to the floor unconscious.

Beaudry holstered his dagger in the diagonal sheath strapped across his chest. He grabbed the boy's feet and dragged him down onto the center aisle. He stood over the boy, glaring at him, then crouched and studied the boy's face while caressing his brow.

Beaudry abruptly stood, returned to the sanctuary floor. He drew his sword from the sheath embedded to the back of his long coat and stood over Daemiana in a high guard defense — arms cocked, wrists locked against his temple, blade horizontally forward. It was as if she were more dangerous than even him.

"As many as I love, I rebuke and chasten; be zealous therefore, and repent."

Absolutely not... Only he and his ilk were in need of repentance. Murderers... L'assassinos... Monsters... With their ancient, barbaric rituals. But there would be no escaping the slayers this time. She was not healing fast enough. She readied to die there in that vile little church.

Two other Inquisitors — Ivers and McConnolly   stormed in and stood over Daemiana as well. Ivers crouched. He slid her hair off her face and wiped away the tears streaming from her terrified eyes.

"The ritual failed cause it's not possessed," McConnolly warned of Daemiana.

"Don't call her *it* to her face."

"We've done all we can, brother."

"We will resume the Rituale Romanum until repentance is attained," Ivers rasped.

"She successfully gave her soul to Satan. Through a pact. That's unbreakable," McConnolly insisted.

"Nothing is unbreakable," Ivers whispered tenderly to Daemiana. "I will break you. You will repent."

"She escaped once; she'll escape again. A Romanum Execution is justified—"

"Simply killing her solves nothing. Breaking her resolves EVERYTHING."

"The longer this drags out, brother, the more we're play'in into her hands. Time's run'in out. Execute her now before she kills the rest of us—"

"I am not sending her soul to hell!" Ivers growled. He again wiped away Daemiana's tears. "She will repent when she is ready. Only then will that be justified."

"Grand Inquisitor..." Daemiana whispered to Ivers. "Leave me be..."

"She's an abomination, brother. Even animals got enough sense to want to destroy her—"

"The mission has always been to save their souls, not slay them with impunity," Ivers said and kissed Daemiana's hand. "We captured one alive, finally. We will now do just that. Save their souls."

"What if she escapes again? What if the others arrive—"

"Let us resume," Ivers ordered sternly. "I do not want it brought up again."

Beaudry's cold, pale, stoic blue eyes had remained locked on Daemiana the entire time, unblinking, indifferent, yet pious and dignified.

"Yes, Monsignor," McConnolly finally conceded.

Ivers pulled a book from his inner coat pocket entitled: THE RITUALE ROMANUM. Daemiana screamed as he opened it to a section entitled: RITUS EXORCIZANDI. Beaudry slammed his foot down onto her chest and tightened his grip on his sword. Ivers pressed a silver cross to her forehead, emitting a loud searing hiss.

Her hysterical screams jerked the boy back into consciousness. Caelin managed to stagger to his feet. He stumbled forward—

Beaudry thrust the butt of his sword into Caelin's stomach and up at his chin in a single fluid motion, then grabbed the boy's throat before he fell and held him up with one hand. Beaudry's speed and prowess were that of a master assassin.

He caressed the boy's mouth with his thumb and yanked him closer.

"The lips of the righteous nourish many, but fools die for lack of sense," Beaudry whispered. He knocked the boy out completely with a headbutt, easing his foot off Daemiana's chest slightly.

She had healed enough to scramble away and pounce to her feet.

She dodged their sword strikes and outran them by leaping over pew after pew after pew until she escaped in a hail of silencer-muffled gunfire.

They gave chase.

Daemiana fled into the open wild, full speed, never once looking back. The boy's diversion had saved her from the Inquisitors. No male had ever saved her, only hurt her. Perhaps, she misjudged him. Perhaps, he was different. Perhaps, they shot him and killed him while she escaped.

Her eyes welled as she left the town far behind. She would never forget his sacrifice. He had served his purpose well, after all. For what he had done, for his courage, she would forever be fondly grateful. She had saved him from the bears; he had saved her from the slayers. The slayers were far worse.

CHAPTER 11

CAELIN GROANED AS HE AWAKENED ON THE ALTER FLOOR. HE STARED at the veiny cracks on the chapel ceiling for a while and regained his senses. Those little cracks were something he would have noticed and fixed if he ever entered the chapel like a normal groundskeeper. It was nice of Father Wallace not to push him too hard. Father Wallace... Wait...

It all came back to him.

Caelin sat up, winced, and clutched his head.

It looked like late afternoon outside.

He then saw the girl's dried blood on the floor. He staggered to his feet and again groaned. His head throbbed with every step. His ribs ached with each breath. He stumbled to the double doors with a growing sense of panic.

Caelin sprinted out of the chapel but abruptly stopped. There was a trail of blood leading into the open wild. He began following it but instead resumed his sprint back to the heart of town for help.

Caelin bolted into the Sheriff's Office and rushed Deputy Bob and Deputy Mike, who were at their desks frantically shouting into their phones.

"H-H-Help!" Caelin pleaded.

He glimpsed the gory investigation photos of dead Sheriff Dollins, Father Wallace, and Dr. Schmidt. They had been torn apart. Caelin screamed.

"No!"

"Thought I told you to stay put, Caelin!" Deputy Bob barked and resumed raging into his phone. "I don't care about storms and rough seas! I don't have a couple of days! I need State Troopers, I need Search & Rescue, I need bear hunters, and I need'em now!"

Deputy Mike was screaming into his phone too.

"I don't give a fuck! We got rabid grizzlies out here or some shit, killing people! We got three dead, including our Sheriff and a missing girl!"

"Deputy B-B-Bob," Caelin gasped.

"Hold on!" both yelled.

"It wasn't bears!" Caelin finally got out. "It was three m-m-men! They did it! I saw them trying to kill the g-g-girl too!"

"What?" they both said.

"They attacked me too!"

"Slow down. What men?" Deputy Bob demanded.

"I-I-I don't know. We gotta stop them before they kill her!"

"Caelin, tell me exactly what happened—"

"There's n-n-no time! I think I know which way they went! Let's go!"

"Hold on! It's just me n' Mike here! No one's going anywhere till we figure out what the hell's go'in on!"

Caelin screamed and paced around, still not thinking straight.

"Caelin, you're in shock. Sit the fuck down and breathe," Deputy Mike said.

Caelin instead stormed out the door.

"Hey! The town's on lockdown!" both yelled but had no choice except to return to their emergency phone calls.

Caelin stormed into Dad's house and paced around, biting his nails. There wasn't much left to bite; he'd been a nailbiter his whole life. So, he nibbled on his fingertips and tried not to lose it completely.

The walls boasted photos of Stephen and Caelin's father-son adventures: rock climbing, fishing, backpacking, horseback riding, hunting, sailing, and mountaineering. Caelin looked strangely awkward and terrified in each because he usually was. Nature was not his natural habitat. He didn't really belong anywhere, to think of it.

He hated those photos. He never really knew who he feared more, nature or his father. They were one and the same.

Caelin found himself somberly staring at the old photo of Dad atop K2 with a big smile on his frost-nipped face. That was a few years before Caelin was born. Who was that man? A stranger? A psycho? A badass with nothing to prove and nothing to lose? All Dad ever wanted was for him to be a man too. That much Caelin knew. Maybe, it was time to start.

Caelin stormed into Dad's supply room. He grabbed a rifle and a backpack with two ice axes affixed to it. He tossed into it: ammo, survival gear, ropes, climbing, and mountaineering gear. He then threw on his mountaineering garb, boots, and headlamp.

He rushed the open wild like a wayward pasture animal. It awaited eagerly past the old chapel at town's edge. He lugged along clumsily, with the rifle in his hands and the gear on his back. It was only the first leg of his naive plight, and he was already tiring. Reality set in harder and faster with every step that took him further from town. The trees eventually engulfed him. The old chapel was no longer visible behind him. Would Dad approve? Or was Caelin in so far over his head that even Dad would tell him to stand down?

The girl's sparse blood trail begged him to press on.

He stumbled along, winded and sweaty. The terrain gradually steepened and roughened. He tripped, fell, and set off the rifle. Its recoil kicked him in the chest like an angry mule. He writhed in pain as his ears rung.

Caelin eventually sat up and stared at the stars in the early dusk sky. Was he out of his mind? He couldn't do this. Even if he found the girl, the three psychos would kill him. They had knives, guns, swords, rifles, and who knows what else. Nothing wrong with letting Deputy Bob and Deputy Mike do their jobs and handle it when they got around to it. All Caelin could do was hope it all turned out okay.

CHAPTER 12

FUCK THAT. CAELIN PERSEVERED AGAINST HIS BETTER JUDGMENT, IF only a little bit longer. It was about baby steps. One step at a time, and before you knew it, you were there, as Dad would say. So Caelin trekked along, beneath the illuming three-quarter moon, through the steep, perilous bush, nearing the foot of the mountains. The blood smudges had grown sparse. He felt more and more bent on finding the girl. The mountains were her only escape.

With crampons affixed to his boots and an ice axe in each gloved hand, Caelin slowly ascended the mountain via a mild, highly exposed ridge. The crunch of each grueling step took him further from his fears, enlivening him until all unease was gone. He was up there alone, as his own man, drawing strength from the breathtaking views of the shimmery coastline far below, beneath the glowing moon. The neighboring peaks egged him on. So, he kept going.

Caelin glimpsed why Dad seemed happiest on a mountain. He was beginning to feel it for the first time ever: the exhilaration of life at its rawest, yet at its purest, at its most potent, and at its most frag-ile, as Dad would say. Only then would one appreciate it most. Caelin felt that elusive rush surging in him. It was the feeling of being too alive to die. Why, oh why, couldn't he have felt it while Dad was still alive? Maybe then, they would have had something in common—

A gust smacked him back into the moment. The winds had picked up deceptively slow.

The winds hit him head-on and full force, threatening to pluck him off the mountain. At elevation, there was nothing to wane them, nothing to warm them, nothing between him and them. The chill pierced him to the bone. He'd forgotten to check the weather before embarking. That was the gravest of all mountaineering sins.

The fear was back. Death was lurking. How quickly it had all become a suicide mission. The point of no return had long passed. Caelin labored not to panic as he continued ascending steadily. If he was going to die, it would not be in retreat. Fuck it, but he sure as shit had picked the wrong time to grow a pair of balls. Dad would've yelled at him for this predicament, no doubt. This was not how you climbed mountains. You laid siege to them as the weather permitted. Errors of omission were just as deadly as errors of commission. Or was it the other way around? Shit. He'd soon be dead and able to ask Dad personally, assuming there was some kind of afterlife, some-thing Caelin had long struggled with, even as death seemed imminent. How'd he get himself into this shit? He was no fucking hero. He was too scared to die. What the fuck had he been thinking? They'd probably never even find his body. Yet, for some reason, inexplicably, he pressed on.

The storm gradually eased, but the burning cold and skinny air continued beating him down. It sapped him of the will to go on. Every few staggery steps, he keeled forward and clutched his knees, gasping for air. He was no longer making much progress. He was freezing to death. But he refused to die there and let Dad's death be in vain at that point. Dad had given his life to save him. He couldn't do that to him. Not there. Caelin fought on. If he were going to die, it'd be on the summit. There at least, it would honor Dad in some small way.

After a long ordeal, he finally staggered onto the broad, stubby summit. Caelin fell to his knees. He threw his arms up victoriously, if only for a moment—his first solo ascent and summit. At night, in less than ideal weather. Tears streamed from his eyes and froze on his cheeks. It was not something he ever wanted, but he took it. The climb had not been too technical, unlike the stuff he and Dad would do, but no one could ever take it away from him. He was a climber.

Caelin stumbled and slid his way down the opposite side of the mountain via another mild yet treacherously exposed ridge. With each weary step, the air seemed less hostile, more breathable. His strength was somewhat returning. He was thinking straight again. It looked more and more like he would not be dying on the mountain that day.

The fabled Alaskan interior wild awaited him. It was colder and meaner and more remote than the coast. Its grizzlies were hungrier. It was where hunters went to hunt death itself. No one lived out here in these badlands as far as he knew, not even Hermit Lawson. But then again, he knew nothing. Wasn't this place where the girl had come from?

Caelin navigated the rugged, interior wild as best he could. He was beyond spent. He had to find a spot to camp for the rest of the night if he survived long enough. Everything there seemed to be colluding to kill him. Pointy rocks lay in wait beneath patches of fluffy snow. Precarious slopes abutted jagged boulders, which seemingly yearned to greet him full force and face first. The exposed roots of shadowy trees schemed to trip him up, to ensure it.

A bloodcurdling howl boomed in the distance. Caelin flinched and looked around. He let loose a panicked bolt for the tallest tree, dropped his gear, and climbed frantically but kept slipping back down. Even after his solo summit, trees were still insurmountable. What the fuck was it with trees? It had always been that way, even before it cost him Dad's life. He was tempted to flee back up the mountain, where he would surely die.

Caelin spotted a huge rock formation in the near distance. He grabbed his gear and bolted for it.

He yanked his rock climbing gear from his pack as he ran up on the rock formation. He secured the harness to himself, strapped an ice axe to his back, coiled a rope around one shoulder, and began climbing, abandoning all else.

The howl boomed closer.

Caelin nearly lost his grip, then his footing, nearly falling and barely recovering each time by sheer luck.

He paused, closed his eyes, took a deep breath.

Stay calm. Always.

He persevered in a slow, steady manner.

After an arduous effort, he crawled onto the top of the formation. He switched off his headlamp and rolled onto his back, drenched in sweat, more spent than ever.

The night had grown oppressively cold. Caelin was shivering, and mist was emanating from his nose with every exhale. The cold rock itself was sapping his body heat. Lying there, still and exposed, was costing him dearly.

Whatever it was that spooked him, though, was gone. All was tranquil. Caelin turned onto his stomach and peered down. He switched on his headlamp. He stared longingly at the rolled mountaineering jacket, sleeping bag, and tent strapped to his pack. He shouldn't have abandoned his gear, much less after removing his mountaineering jacket while trudging through the interior, beginning to overheat. Abandoning his gear in a panic had been a stupid move, yet something typical of him. It's why Dad insisted that he always remain calm. Always. Calm. Believe it. When was he going to learn?

Caelin secured his belay and abseiled halfway down. He hung on the line clumsily, laboring to scope the area. The rock formation and trees obscured most of the moonlight. His headlamp was dimming. He had to change the batteries. But nothing seemed out of the ordinary.

He abseiled all the way to the ground. Before he could grab his gear—

Mist emanated from a nearby boulder; beautiful, billowy, whiter than white rising from pitch black.

Caelin stared at it, frozen.

He was forcing his eyes to discern what it was.

It wasn't a boulder.

He couldn't move, even as he finally discerned the mist to be emanating from a huge, diabolically incensed snout.

It charged.

Caelin scrambled back up the rock formation as it rose onto its hind legs and leapt at him. It clawed the soles of his boots as it smashed into the rock.

Caelin arrested his fall by holding on to the line for dear life. He frantically resumed climbing.

It did it all over again and again, smashing violently into the vertical rock, unable to climb up after him.

Caelin eventually crawled onto the top in hysterics.

It tore at the rock formation until its claws penetrated the rock itself. It began climbing.

Caelin got off belay and fumbled down the opposite side.

When most of the way down, he jumped and hit the ground running.

He snaked around trees and boulders, leaped over downed logs, dove into dense shrubbery, crawled through, and resumed his frantic sprint.

The pursuing growls were devolving into a macabre dissonance of seething, diabolic fury, like some overture of death. Just then—

Caelin scrambled to a frenzied stop, slipping, falling, and sliding toward something just as horrific. It was the scar-faced bear. How'd it get from the coast to the interior?!

Caelin curled into a ball and was sprayed with blood as the grizzly and the demonic fury tore into one another. The swivels of claws and teeth were so ferocious; even the ground beneath was being torn apart.

Caelin crawled away from the warring monsters.

Three shadowy figures were grimly converging, swords in hand, appearing to have tracked one or both monstrosities. They bore mountaineering garb and gear and headlamps. It was the three psychos. Had they traversed the mountains too?

"Thou shall not eateth bloody flesh; neither shall ye use enchantments or practice sorcery...," Beaudry preached as McConnolly thrust his sword at the demonic fury.

 It dodged the blade and dropped a thunderous claw to his chest — to a loud searing hiss — that sent McConnolly flying back.

Beaudry lunged at it, dodged its claw strikes, then thrust his sword into its heart, emitting a loud searing hiss. It fled.

The bear, Beaudry, and McConnolly gave chase.

Caelin remained on the ground, clutching his pounding chest with one hand and his ice axe with the other.

What the fuck...?

The demonic fury had looked part animal, part person, draped in red—

"Foolish boy!" Ivers growled as he stood over Caelin. "Why are you here?!"

"W-W-W-W-What was that...?"

"A bear."

"The other one—"

"Rabid bears! Like the ones that killed your father! Go home before they kill you too!"

"That w-w-wasn't a bear—"

"It was."

"It wasn't! I saw it!"

"Such things do not exist..." Ivers rasped.

"I s-s-saw it—"

"...because things like that are eradicated. By us."

"What?"

"Go home!"

"W-W-Where's the girl?"

"There is no girl."

"I'm here to save her l-l-life!"

Ivers glared at the love bites on Caelin's neck, displeased.

"That was the girl," he groaned ominously. "Forget her. Go home and urge the town to evacuate. Tell them: the bears have gone rabid, and more are on the way. Then, pray for us all."

"Y-Y-You're crazy! That wasn't the girl! She saved m-m-my life! You can't kill her! She's just a scared girl!"

"Heroism makes martyrs, boy. Prayer is safer. GO HOME," Ivers warned menacingly, then stormed off into the night.

Caelin hesitated, then retreated the way he came, heeding the warning.

He eventually slowed to a stop.

He turned, again hesitated, and instead followed Ivers to certain death. He couldn't let those three psychos kill her. They were out of their minds, and she needed his help.

CHAPTER 13

IVERS RESUMED THE HUNT IN TURMOIL, NO LONGER SURE WHETHER he was pursuing the anomaly or fleeing the boy's foolish aim. The boy now threatened everything. Laypeople were not to know of *the situation*; they were only to be protected from it. And if someone knew, all would soon know. The Order could not have that. Those who would not be kept in the dark were to be silenced by it.

But Ivers had again proven himself unfit when he failed to slay the boy out of an abundance of caution. It was an antiquated practice he no longer could abide. Ivers had become too wedged between ire and empathy for the kid. He understood the boy's naive plight better than the boy would ever know. And it opened old wounds in Ivers, over the nature of choice, about the nature of love, over what happened with Isabella.

For such was a solitary life when it was closer to the end than it was the beginning; when one could only sift through the past for meaning and mine it for peace, only to find that one's fervors were too amiss, for far too long. And that one's victories were too unbeknown, to too many, to reap any joy. Life was messy. Happiness was serendipitous. Peace was elusive, if not outright unattainable. Caution, therefore, best belonged in the wind, as the boy had done in his quest to save the girl. Ivers almost envied the boy's zeal. Let it all be known, to each his own! Which begged the question, had Ivers abandoned too hastily his passion for Isabella? And had that choice cost him his happiness?

These tortured musings and convoluted inner ramblings mauled Ivers as he traversed the nocturne wild, rendering him more and more futile. He was once the greatest of all slayers, though all too often guided by wrath rather than mercy, and at his worst, was more interested in spilling blood than saving souls. He was no longer fit to do either.

The werewolf had long escaped, yet Ivers persevered, clinging to his dignity until his old body said no more. He aborted the pursuit and veered in a new direction.

He arrived at the rendezvous before dawn. Nestled among dense trees and shrubbery, beneath a canopy of thick, overlying foliage, was a downed, moss-covered log. Deep in its hollow was a weapon and supply cache.

Ivers wiped the sweat from his face before it turned clammy. Beyond the safety of the river cabin and its surroundings, this area was near ideal. Close quarters combat favored the Order. While a life-saving brook was not too far for a drink, its life-threatening rustle was not too close so as to dampen the sound of an approaching threat.

Ivers dropped his weighty rucksack, exhausted. It was gorged with mountaineering and survival gear. He paced around, still brooding. Should he have killed the girl when he had the chance? The stakes were too high. Too many lives were on the line. Too many lives had already been lost. Too much blood was already on his hands. The regret, the uncertainty, the waffling, his hastening decline. It had to be curbed and mitigated—

McConnolly arrived and signaled that the three-quarter werewolf had escaped them too. Three-quarter, like the moon that night, to which it was beholden.

"Ya alright, Monsignor?"

Ivers nodded.

"Alas, we did not return emptyhanded," McConnolly grinned

Beaudry emerged with a deer carcass draped over his shoulders.

The deer crackled over the fire. Ivers ate in silence. They all did. His 45-year tenure with the Order was near over. He was 65. Beaudry was in his 40s. McConnolly was in his 30s. Either was young enough to be his son, yet neither was ready to lead. As skilled as they were, they were nearly as unfit as him. Lurking beneath Beaudry's pious fervor was darkness. A darkness Ivers could sense. Beaudry was fleeing deeper and deeper into piety. McConnolly ailed from the opposite extreme, an impious care for only the thrill of the hunt. He was a spiritual bounty hunter, God's contract killer, and increasingly ever merciless. Ivers had tragically embodied both self-righteous extremes in his youth. Those dark days were thankfully behind him, vanquished by the humbling pangs of time. Ivers hoped the same for them; that their faults would wither with age as well—

A faint snap swooped them to their feet with guns and daggers drawn, forearms plumb, exhibiting the lethal modernity of commandos and the swordsmanship of medieval knights, able to shoot and stab adeptly and simultaneously.

It was not the werewolf. If it were, it would have already ripped into them. It could only be that, "Stupid boy!" Ivers growled. "I said go home and evacuate the town!"

For some reason, Ivers found himself grinning for the first time in a long time. It was all devolving into what he had feared: chaos. Yet, Ivers was as amused as he was livid. The boy had been undeterred by what he barely survived, just to save the girl.

"So you chose martyrdom," Ivers quipped. "Quite noble."

Beaudry and McConnolly glared at Ivers.

"Monsignor, he is a loose end," McConnolly warned.

"He will return home, unharmed," Ivers ordered.

McConnolly scoffed and paced in riled disbelief.

"Young Caelin," McConnolly mocked. "The chapel groundskeeper who never sets foot in his chapel! Welcome. No martyr should die on an empty stomach, brother. Not even one who's got a damned quarrel with God!"

"I don't have a quarrel w-w-with anyone," the boy snapped back. McConnolly's words had struck a nerve.

"Life gave ya a bad hand. Your misguided good deeds won't change that," McConnolly pressed him.

"God gave m-m-me a bad hand," Caelin ominously replied and ventured into the open. "Or maybe it was just Karma. Whatever you want to call it."

The slayers were taken aback by Caelin's rancorous blasphemy.

"If *He* is so bad, brother, why do ya volunteer as chapel groundskeeper?" McConnolly demanded to know.

"You don't n-n-need a God to be charitable—"

"For the eyes of the Lord behold all the earth, and give strength to those who with a perfect heart trust in Him. Wherefore thou hast done foolishly, and for this cause from this time, wars shall arise against thee," Beaudry warned.

Caelin simply stared at him bewildered.

"II Chronicles 16," Ivers said. "Father Beaudry's vow is one of silence. He occasionally speaks, in Biblical passages only."

"Wh-Wh-Where is she?" the boy wasted no time in asking.

"She has devoured men far mightier than you," Ivers replied. "As she did those at the clinic. Only we are equipped to handle situations like *hers*. Go home and urge the town to evacuate. NOW. More of her kind may soon arrive."

"I don't believe in m-m-monsters."

"Well, maybe ya damn well should, brother!" McConnolly exploded.

"In matters of the Church, what you believe, matters not," Ivers warned Caelin.

The boy stepped forward, still undeterred.

"Then, let the Bishop decide. I called him a-a-after Father Wallace died. He's on his way to town—"

Beaudry's dagger swooshed past Caelin's head and lodged in an adjacent tree.

"Just a warning," McConnolly advised.

Ivers sighed. There would be no happy ending for the boy. His heart would either be broken by the truth or ripped out by it.

Caelin stared down at the ground for a while, his denial appearing to crack.

"Is there a cure?" he asked, finally appearing to acknowledge the situation.

Still, his lingering naivety served as a stark reminder of the grave danger. The boy, like the modern world, would never accept that there existed no bodily cure for the affliction, only a spiritual one.

"She is a feral darling," Ivers rasped. "For which there is no cure."

"Are y-y-you gonna kill her?"

If Ivers' response were to be too harsh, it would provoke the boy to continue his foolish crusade and lead to his eventual death. If Ivers' response were too weak, it would further fuel McConnolly's defiance. A balanced response was paramount.

"Yes," Ivers said.

McConnolly nodded, clearly wanting to hear it.

"Humanely, and in a manner that will not send her soul to hell," Ivers was compelled to add. Which meant the exorcisms would continue until she repented. And that was *not* what McConnolly wanted to hear.

"I trust before her coven arrives n' kills us all, Monsignor," McConnolly replied with restrained contempt. "Then again, when you give your soul to Satan via a pact, hell's exactly what you deserve."

"Thank you, Brother McConnolly," Ivers rasped, holding his stare until McConnolly looked away.

But Ivers' doubts lingered like overzealous gastric juice. His command dangled precariously like iced snot on a frostbitten corpse. Who was right? He, the boy, or McConnolly? In his youth, Ivers would have killed them all outright: the girl for being what she was, the boy and McConnolly for crossing him, and anyone else unfortunate enough to get in his way. God help him. God help them all.

CHAPTER 14

"Eat," Ivers ordered.

"Wh-Wh-What?"

"Before you go."

The old psycho didn't seem to be asking as he gestured for Caelin to sit at the fire with them.

"Go wh-wh-where?"

"Back home, boy! Where do you think? After you eat."

Caelin glanced at the deer crackling on the fire. His stomach was grumbling with hunger, but Caelin had no intention of going anywhere till he figured out how to stop them from killing the girl. He couldn't let it go. There had to be another way.

"Now!" Ivers growled.

Caelin complied. If there were going to kill him, they would have done so already. So he approached and sat at the fire with them, unsure what to say, uncertain what to do, not sure how to act. It was not unlike any other interaction in his life, social or otherwise. He was just plain awkward and did not fit in anywhere, even there, in the remote interior wild, where there was no pretense. Everything was as it simply was. Yet, he couldn't quite fit there either. It weighed on him.

The three psychos were devouring their slabs of meat in silence. He knew better than to speak, the way he knew better than to disturb a large dog while it fed. They were killers. That much he was sure of as he stared into the fire.

The jostling flames reflected as flickery, orange gleams against their shiny weaponry, further cautioning him not to fuck with them. Silver guns were holstered to their ankles and hips. Silver bullet clips lined their belts. Silver daggers were sheathed diagonally across their chests. Silver swords were sheathed vertically down their backs, parallel to the silver rifles strapped to their backs. Caelin's eyes lingered most on the silvery glimmer of the armor lining the inside of their long, brown coats. All that shit because of a girl?

McConnolly suddenly drew his sword as he jumped to his feet and swung it at the deer carcass head, lopping it off in a swift, fluid swoosh.

Caelin cowered back.

"Only way to kill a Coven Werewolf, brother, in case you were wonder'in," he said to Caelin. "Except during a full moon, of course, when it's almost impossible, cause it's fully shifted, n' it's just too big, too fast, too strong. At that point, ya just run n' hide n' try to survive the bloody fuck'in night."

"Language," Ivers warned.

McConnolly carved off a big slab of deer meat and tossed it at Caelin.

"So ya see, we're in a race against time here. Eat."

The meat scalded Caelin's hands. He dropped it onto his lap and tried to grasp it as it burned his lap too.

"I-I-I'm a vegetarian..."

Beaudry was just glaring at Caelin, never once blinking.

"Well, ya little girlfriend isn't, brother. That I can promise ya," McConnolly laughed. "Eat!"

"Enough," Ivers said.

Caelin glared at his meat, doing his best to ignore the burning pain, not wanting to give them the satisfaction of seeing him drop it. They clearly thought he was a joke, like everyone else. He was sick of being pushed around his whole life. Every nasty memory was bubbling to the surface. He'd gotten used to the taunting and the ridicule, but the ass-kickings, the physical pain, there was no getting used to that.

Lori's boyfriend was the bully back home. His rule was a punch for every stutter. So Caelin never spoke around the guy, no matter how much the guy insisted it'd cure his speech impediment.

 McConnolly was the new bully. They all were. But Caelin wasn't going to take it anymore.

"Wh-Wh-What's her name?" Caelin asked, knowing it'd irk them. His way of sticking it back to them. It worked.

"Her *name*, brother? Try *it*. Cause it has no bloody fuck'in name!"

"Enough!" Ivers growled. "Don't call her *it*."

The silence was tense.

Nerves and hunger drove Caelin to nibble at his meat. He wasn't all that vegetarian. He tried to be, most of the time. It's just that meat wasn't good for one's Karma.

"Daemiana," Ivers sighed as he stared into the fire.

Caelin locked eyes with him. Was that her name?

"A beautiful name for a beautiful girl. As in life, things are often not as they seem. Do you understand, boy? In our zeal, sometimes we make errors in judgment. The consequences of which can be life-long. Do you understand? You are making such errors, NOW. I pray you will never come to know the weight of immense regret on your shoulders. That is why you will journey back home at sunrise, find a way to evacuate the town, and forget her. A feral darling is incapable of love. Do you understand?"

McConnolly was scraping meat from between his teeth with the tip of his dagger. He spit, leaned in, glared at Caelin.

"Heard your old man was tough on ya. Mine was too. Think maybe it's why I hunt monsters," McConnolly seemed to ponder aloud. "But no matter how many I slay, I never measure up. He's been dead over 10 years, and I'm still hunt'in. Guess what I'm say'in is, ya sure ya ain't out here play'in hero, try'in to impress the ghost of ya dear old dad?"

Caelin watched the fire prance and bounce and weave while trying to tune them out. But he couldn't. When they weren't being assholes, they made some sense. Not that they had him all figured out or anything. What the fuck did they know?

"It's a shit life, brother. I don't recommend it."

Ivers stood and approached the downed, moss-covered log. He reached inside the cache and pulled out a bundle, then tossed it at Caelin's feet. It was a sheathed silver dagger and a long, brown, hooded coat. Both were exactly like theirs.

"For your protection, on your journey back home," Ivers said, again not asking. "You will not survive another night out here. Things will get exponentially worse."

CHAPTER 15

FIRST LIGHT BEAMED, LETTING CAELIN KNOW THAT HE SOMEHOW survived the night. His new coat felt heavy on him, like an armored poncho. The sheathed dagger was strapped diagonally across his chest, handle up, as they wore it. They had shown him how to yank it out and slash in a single motion.

He looked back at them. They weren't asking. He had to go. Caelin was to return the way he came and arrive back home alive to evacuate the town. They were so insistent about evacuation. They instructed him to say: *Rabid grizzlies had killed not only Dad but everyone at the clinic. And more were out there.*

"Hurry home, brother. Her nightly shapeshift gets more n' more complete as the moon cycle progresses," McConnolly warned Caelin while glaring at Ivers. "Three nights till the full moon, Monsignor. Even the bears got enough sense to run n' hide during the full moon."

That final thought mauled at Caelin's gut as he fled.

"We had better find her then, Brother McConnolly," Ivers ordered. "Soon."

McConnolly watched Caelin flee. He then crouched and pensively ran his hands over Caelin's tracks.

Caelin eventually arrived back at the rock formation. The sight of the hideous claw marks on the rock turned his stomach. It had really happened! He had almost died.

Caelin quickly retrieved the gear he had abandoned and resumed his trek back home. He didn't get far before he stopped and turned. He gazed back at the rock formation as if it were calling him. He should have ignored it.

Caelin climbed up onto the top of the rock formation, winded and sweaty.

He was searching the distance meticulously, in all directions, with his binoculars. After a while, he froze. His lips quivered.

Daemiana was frolicking in a lake. She was nude, graceful, happy, free, mesmerizing. Everything he wasn't. Everything he yearned for. He lowered the binoculars before he got too hard. There had to be another way than what the three psychos wanted to do to her. A cure had to exist. It just had to.

Caelin eventually arrived at the lakeshore in a waddling sprint, lugging all his gear, drenched in sweat, lungs burning. He looked around, more exhilarated than tired. Daemiana was gone. He turned and turned, searching. The thought of never seeing her again ached. It nauseated him. Or maybe it was the exhaustion setting in from sprinting about a mile with the full weight of his gear on him—a stupid move. Mountaineers knew better than to fatigue themselves before an ascent. Exhaustion killed. Caelin clutched his head, feeling the self-loathing return. He had fucked up again. When was he finally going to learn?

Without a sound, Daemiana emerged atop a boulder above him. Her long cloak eerily flapped in the breeze. She leapt and landed behind him with animal-like silence and agility. She enshrouded her nude body with the cloak.

"You deceived me."

Caelin spun around and nearly fell, beyond startled at the sight of her. The thought of how weak it must have looked agonized him. He refused to be weak in her eyes.

She circled him, caressing each tree she passed while glaring at his long, brown, armored coat and silver dagger.

Caelin quickly realized how that must have looked to her.

"N-N-No—"

"Unkilled by the slayers?" she asked with pleasant surprise or disappointment; he wasn't quite sure.

"What?"

"You said you would help me."

"I w-w-will."

"You are one of them."

"I'm n-n-not."

She quit strolling about and hugged a tree.

"How can I trust him?" she appeared to ask the tree.

"I helped you. Back a-a-at the chapel—"

"I cannot trust him. Can I?" she asked the tree again.

"You talk to trees?"

"Once, I was in harmony with nature. Now, Mother hates me. Because of what I am."

What she was? She was perfect; that's what she was, beyond beautiful. But he couldn't help wondering, "What are you?" he finally said, after some hesitation, conceding to his better judgment that perfection didn't exist. It was unattainable, at least for guys like him—

"*What are you?*" she replied defensively.

Daemiana approached him faster than he could step back. She ran her sharp nails over his dagger, appearing both frightened and intrigued. She seemed to like him more. But why, if she thought him dangerous? Women had always been impossible to understand.

"You don't have to be scared of m-m-me—"

"I would never be scared of *you*."

"They m-m-made me wear it," he admitted before he could stop himself. Why did he phrase it that way? Especially after her insulting tone. Was she calling him a pussy?

"Do you always do as others tell you?" she asked, again with the insulting tone.

"N-N-No," he stammered.

"I do not believe you."

Caelin just looked down. Was she bullying him now too?

"What else did they tell you?"

He fixed his sights back on her, deciding not to take it anymore.

"They told me everything," he fired back.

"Did they?"

Not really. They had told him almost nothing now that he thought about it.

She resumed hugging the tree.

"The smell of this place makes me happy," she said as she closed her eyes and inhaled deeply. "Piney loamy."

What was that her way of changing the subject?

"Can you smell it?" she asked.

Not really. While Kreuger Sound smelled oceany and fishy, the interior probably smelled piney. It only made sense.

"M-M-Maybe cause all the pines?"

"The soil is so alive."

"And the pines," he said. "Like the one you're hugging."

"What is this place?" she asked out of nowhere, stumping him.

Didn't she know? Wasn't this her home?

"Uh... The Interior. A-A-Alaska."

"The Inquisitors brought me to this land to separate me from mine. To use its nature against me."

What...? He noticed that the tree seemed to be slowly wilting. The one she was hugging. Daemiana let go, looking more sorrowed than surprised. Her eyes welled with tears.

What was going on?

"Yet, I fear only the Inquisitors can help me," she conceded.

Now he was beyond confused.

"Help y-y-you? Those three psychos?"

"By breaking the cursed pact which has so deeply offended Mother."

What pact? What mother?

"I do not want to be like this! I do not want to be what I am."

"You don't w-w-wanna be what?"

"An abomination."

Caelin's stomach sank, unsure if he ever really, truly believed it until then. The tree had stopped wilting when she had stepped away from it.

"It is why I sought their help."

"Their help? Y-Y-You let those guys catch you?"

"I will risk anything to find a cure," she replied with no hesitation. "I will go anywhere; I will do anything. The Inquisitors believe they can break the pact, but they failed. It is time to move on and continue searching for a cure."

Caelin clutched his brow, trying to grasp it all. He was in way over his head—

She hugged him tightly. She was all over the place. Did she hate him or like him? She was so soft and smelled so good, yet she could probably kill him anytime with her sharp nails. She had fought the bears and saved his life. The same bears that killed the strongest man he had ever known — Dad. Then last night, the biggest, scariest bear and the three psychos had saved him from *her*. The lines were so blurred.

He hugged her back. His eyes slowly closed as he buried his nose in her silky, burgundy locks. Her sagebrush-like scent relaxed and invigorated him.

"Where the Inquisitors failed, you will succeed," she whispered and sealed her plea for help with a kiss. "I know it."

Caelin nodded boldly, feeling like a real man. He loved how she did that. She made him feel strong. Everyone and everything else made him feel like a feckless weakling. Not her, not in those moments, moments he never wanted to end. She again kissed him and lured his tongue into her mouth, where she gently and affectionately nipped at it with her teeth.

He knew how he would save her and make her his.

"Maybe the bishop can help. For sure, he won't try to kill you like those three psychos—"

She suddenly slipped from his arms as a misty red warmth hit him, just before the sound of the rifle blast did, which left his ears muted and ringing. He plummeted into dread as he fell to his knees, grasped her head, and frantically tried to stop the bleeding. She had been shot.

"No! No!! No!!!" Caelin screamed.

"Fear not them which kill the body, but cannot kill the soul. Instead, fear him who is able to destroy both body and soul in hell," Beaudry preached, rifle in hand, approaching from behind.

"No!"

"Had a feel'in, you'd lead us straight to her, brother," McConnolly said as he violently yanked Daemiana away from Caelin and tossed her up and over his shoulder.

"No!"

"Stop whine'in. She's incapable of love. She's just use'in ya. N' we just saved ya from her, again."

"She's not some animal you can just kill!" Caelin jumped to his feet and tried to wrestle Daemiana away—

Beaudry smashed the butt of the rifle into the back of his head, knocking him out.

"For we account a man to be justified by faith, without the works of the law."

CHAPTER 16

Caelin woke, facedown in the muck. The piney loam permeated his nose and mouth. She was right. The soil was piney too. He spit it out and rubbed his gashed head. The burning throb was there to stay. He could only laugh to flank the sobs. The last ass-kicking this bad had been in grade school. He really had forgotten his lunch money.

Caelin turned onto his back and sat up. The pulsing agony spread to his temples. The self-loathing — for being unable to protect her — agonized him most.

They were long gone with her. Deeper into the interior, no doubt. He grabbed his gear, stumbled to his feet, and resumed his trek, the opposite way, back to the mountains. He couldn't do this alone. He needed the help of someone as crazy as the three psychos. If she was still alive, he had to find her.

Caelin ascended the mountain via the same treacherously exposed ridge in mild, daytime weather.

After another slog, he summitted faster than last time. The feat would've been a bigger deal to him if not for everything that had happened, everything he had seen. Nothing would ever be the same. He found himself questioning everything. But it had happened, of that he was sure. Monsters of all kinds did exist.

He descended back toward the coast, but he ventured off the mild ridge down a steeper, more treacherous ridge at mid-mountain. He descended it slowly and shakily into the rugged, desolate bush of an eerie valley wedged between the coast and the interior, mainly enclosed by mountains. They called it Lawson's bowl. Caelin had no intention of returning home to Kreuger Sound. Nothing was left for him there, no future, no anything.

Dusk loomed as he neared a drab wooden shack overrun with brush and cobwebs. Elk antlers hung over the door as if the place were some uneaten carcass. Caelin slowed to a stop, well shy of it.

Hermit Lawson had always been an almost mythical figure. A scary loner who lived out in the middle of nowhere, who rarely left his valley, eating anything he could kill. Even as Lawson carried him back home that awful day, Caelin half expected to wind up on his dinner plate instead of back home in Kreuger Sound. But after everything that had happened since, after all he'd seen, that fear of Hermit Lawson was gone—

A rifle shot whizzed past Caelin's head.

"That ain't even half of what I got, bitch!"

Caelin hit the ground and covered his head.

"Who goes there, goddamn it? No more warn'in shots, cocksuck-er!"

"It's m-m-me! Don't shoot!"

"Jesus H. Christ, Caelin! I almost fuck'in killed ya! What ya do'in all the way out here by yourself?"

He was again terrified of Lawson.

A flickery oil lamp on a flimsy table barely illuminated the inside of the shack. Caelin was stomaching a leathery venison supper with Lawson as the lamp's bouncy light sparred with the darkness. Many trophy heads hung on the walls: grizzly, moose, wolf, fox, and even walrus.

Caelin swallowed the last of his food and tried to refocus.

"So, that's wh-wh-why I came, Mr. Lawson. I need your help—"

"Good, huh boy," he said and helped himself to seconds. "Deer meat'll put some hair on your chest."

"I came cause y-y-you're the best tracker there is."

"Yeah, well..." he grumbled and finished his meal in silence, oc-casionally sipping moonshine from a filthy jar. When done, he lit and puffed on his pipe. He pensively rubbed the chin somewhere beneath his bushy beard. Lawson finally grimaced.

"That's gotta be the craziest fuck'in story I ever heard. N' I heard some tall ones in my day."

"Those three psychos will kill her if w-w-we don't save her."

"Men with swords chase'in a naked gal?"

"Well, she has a...cape thing. You know, to cover u-u-up."

"In this Alaskan cold? Caelin, if ya could just hear yourself."

"I'm telling the truth! Who do think gave m-m-me this badass knife and coat?"

"The gal?"

"The three psychos!"

"Uh-huh. Look. You lost your daddy not long ago. To fuck'in grizzlies. Shit like that'll fuck you in the head. You're in mourn'in, is all. You had a nightmare."

"This is real!"

"I believe that you believe that—"

"You gotta help m-m-me. We can save her! I know we can! We'll take your guns!"

Lawson laughed and smacked Caelin on the shoulder.

"Tomorrow, I'm tak'in ya back home, kid. Time to sleep it off."

Caelin brooded on the floor in his sleeping bag. He didn't quite know who were worse, dozers or dissers, as he called them. Dozers bulldozed over him. Dissers dismissed him altogether. All because he was so weak and pathetic. He had figured Mr. Lawson for a dozer all these years. Not that he knew him well enough to know for sure. But Mr. Lawson had just dismissed him and everything he said. Dozers — the bullies of the world — took him seriously enough to kick his ass, as the three psychos had. Dissers, on the other hand, Caelin decided, were worse. They didn't even feel he, or anything he had to say, were worth a second thought. Mr. Lawson, it turned out, was a disser. Fuck him.

And who the fuck hunted walrus anyway? And why the hell put animal heads on your walls? And who the fuck lived in a shack in the middle of nowhere? And who cared? He was losing precious time. How was he going to convince this asshole to help him? Cause he wasn't going back home, no matter what. He couldn't. There was nothing to go back to. They were all dead. Dad, Father Wallace, Dr. Schmidt, Sheriff Dollins. It was all just too much to face. There was no going back to life as he knew it. It was over.

Caelin wiped his glistening eyes and glanced over at the door, where Lawson was, staring out, puffing on his pipe, and sipping moonshine. Lawson lived alone, happy. He didn't need a town. Maybe it wasn't that bad. Maybe bagging walruses alone in the middle of nowhere was all anyone needed in life. Maybe he could become be a hermit too, away from all the dozers and dissers in the world. But then, who would save Daemiana?

CHAPTER 17

A SHOTGUN WAS COCKED.

Lawson awoke.

The barrel was aimed at his face. Caelin was at the other end, clutching the weapon with trembly hands.

"Boy, you're way outta line."

Caelin was undeterred.

"Gimme it," Lawson ordered.

"I-I-I'm tired of being blown off like the village idiot."

"Put that fuck'in piece down before ya hurt yourself."

"You're gonna h-h-help me find the girl."

"Not gonna happen."

Caelin fired the shotgun at the walrus head, blowing it apart, tusks and all.

Lawson seemed more amenable to the notion.

The overcast dawn was lightening from black to gray.

Lawson emerged from the shack with his hands over his head. Caelin walked behind him, shotgun aimed at his back.

"That's far e-e-enough."

"Nah, I think the gal's this way."

"N-N-No, stop."

Old Lawson kept walking, forcing Caelin to follow.

"I said stop!"

Lawson subtly stepped over something, which Caelin failed to notice, and stepped into it. A rope snared and yanked his ankle up from under him, flipping him over as it thrust him up so violently, the shotgun slipped from his hands.

Caelin dangled upside down, helpless, remembering too late that Lawson was also a master trapper.

"Boy, no man ever pointed a gun at me n' lived," Lawson casually said and grabbed his shotgun off the ground.

Caelin clutched his face as Lawson took aim and fired at the rope from which Caelin was dangling.

Caelin hit the ground headfirst.

Caelin was digging a big hole as Lawson looked on, holding the shotgun like a prison warden, with the barrel over his shoulder.

"Don't kill me, Mr. Lawson. I'm s-s-sorry—"

"Shut up!" Lawson roared. "N' dig faster!"

Caelin dug slowly to bide himself more time before what seemed like his imminent execution and burial in the hole he was digging.

He'd been right in fearing Lawson. Lawson was a killer like the three psychos, which was why he had sought out his help to save the girl after all. But pointing the shotgun at Lawson had turned out to be a huge mistake.

"I'm just trying to save a-a-a girl's life—"

"Every man who crossed me had his reasons."

"But—"

"I live out here alone, to be left alone."

"I'm sorry. I'll n-n-never bother you again—"

"Fuck'in dig!"

So that was it. Hermit Lawson — not the grizzlies, not the three psychos, not the feral darling — would be the end of him.

The big hole was finished.

Caelin was facing it, too numb to sob as Lawson stood behind him.

"Anything ya gotta say, boy?"

There were no words.

"Well then, pray. Now's the time."

"P-P-Pray?"

"Now's the fuck'in time!" Lawson roared again. "Pray!"

Caelin's terror gave way to a flash of anger. Pray to who? To give thanks for what, some short, shit life?! And everyone else was dead;

maybe the girl too! He had failed in every way. Caelin was ready to go. Fuck it all.

"Well?!" Lawson demanded.

"I don't pray to anyone or anything."

As much as Caelin wanted to die like a man, he failed. The tears streamed as he closed his eyes tightly and braced himself.

"What the fuck ya wait'in for?!" Lawson again demanded.

Caelin clenched his jaw, readying for it all to go black forever.

"I gotta take my morning dump, already! And the old shit hole's full!"

What?

Caelin slowly opened his eyes. He looked back at Lawson.

"Old native custom, Goddamn it! Ya thank the earth god after dig'in a new shit hole!" Lawson barked. "Ya know damn well! Thank the earth god so we can move the outhouse over this new hole; otherwise, it's bad luck!"

Had Lawson lost his fucking mind? Or had Lawson just been fucking with him the whole time? So, this was the extent of his punishment, digging a new shit hole? And praising the earth god? And worst of all, losing precious time in the quest to save Daemiana?

"Fuck you!" Caelin erupted, unable to remember ever being more furious. "Fuck you!!"

CHAPTER 18

CAELIN STORMED INTO LAWSON'S SHACK. HE GRABBED HIS GEAR AND blew out of there. He was determined to go it alone as he had his whole life. After all, he'd been the friendless only-child to a broken mother and absent father before becoming the isolated only-child to a dead mother, and extreme sportsman-dad bent on making up for lost time. That was until the rogue bears, the three psychos, and Daemiana had changed that for better or worse, leaving him a feckless fool in pursuit of the unattainable. He felt more alone than ever. Or maybe it was all he deserved for being such a loser. Or just maybe, he needed Daemiana more than she needed him.

"I said, help me move the goddamned outhouse!" Lawson raged as Caelin rushed past him. Caelin took satisfaction in seeing how Lawson liked being blown off like some moron.

Lawson fired the shotgun into the air.

"Final warn'in!"

"I'm gonna save the girl w-w-with or without you!"

"Don't fuck'in test me!"

"I'm leaving!"

"To find that goddamned imaginary girlfriend of yours?!"

That's what he thought? The only girls in Caelin's life had to be imaginary? Caelin swung around, charged back.

"She's real, fucker! Fuck you!"

Lawson grinned. He finally nodded.

"Okay, then."

Okay, what?!

"Bout time ya grew a pair n' said it like ya meant it," Lawson added. "Never did trust anyone who lacked conviction."

What was he saying?

"Fuck it. I'll go."

Caelin stared at him in disbelief.

Lawson sternly pointed at the hole.

"After ya help me move the outhouse over my new shit hole. So I can take my morn'in dump."

Lawson exited his newly moved outhouse, buttoning up his pants.

Caelin was studying a map.

"The interior?"

"Y-Y-Yeah—"

"That's where fools n' bad ideas go to die."

Caelin had barely survived that fucking truth.

"Not that it ever stopped me from go'in," Lawson grinned and fastened his belt.

"I know a good w-w-way over the mountains."

"Why the hell would we go over them mountains?"

Caelin stared at him, perplexed, as Lawson yanked a weather-beaten tarp off a rusty metal heap abutting his shack. An old ATV? He'd never seen Lawson ride around on it. Judging by how old it was, he probably hadn't in forever.

They embarked on the screeching rig. Lawson was driving, and Caelin was on the back, both in full gear. They barely heard one another over the engine noise.

"Can this thing m-m-make it?!"

"Easiest way to the interior ain't over them damn mountains!"

"Dad never m-m-mentioned it!"

"It's hell of a lot further; less direct! Most people dunno 'bout it!"

"How?!"

"Ask the grizzlies! It's how some been known to migrate back n' forth!"

"G-G-Grizzlies?"

"Your old man always preferred the high ground, be'in a climber! Maybe it's why he never told ya about it!"

That did explain how the scar-faced bear that killed Dad had gotten from the coast to the interior. But that was impossible. Lawson had to be mistaken.

They sped through the rugged wild of the valley for a long while, paralleling the meandering river at its heart, which flowed the opposite way toward the sea eventually. They veered away gradually, venturing deeper and deeper into the valley's narrowing and steadily ascending, outermost edge—where the snowline grinned in the distance. Somehow it looked off, no longer feeling right. An ominous something seemed to await them.

"W-W-What's that up ahead?"

But Lawson seemed to be done talking.

They navigated the increasing patches of snow and frost-slicked rocks, occasionally getting stuck and pushing the rig through the slush, eventually crossing the snowline.

They finally arrived at an ice cavern amid enormous ice spires. Caelin's gut knotted. The spires were deadly seracs, and the cavern's white void was the womb of death. The place was where the glacial torrents of converging mountain ranges merged into one gigantic glacier. Dad had warned Caelin about places like these, where massive ice sheets ground together and inched up onto one another over months and years and decades, crushing upward into leaning, castle-sized seracs, on the verge of toppling. The place was a radiant death palace. It stood before them, as gatekeeper, between that furthermost edge of the valley and the interior. It was becoming clear Lawson wanted to do what Dad had expressly taught Caelin to avoid at all costs: the traversing of glacial fracture zones. If the underlying crevasses didn't *get* you, the toppling overhead seracs would.

"N-N-No way," Caelin said.

"Here she is. The secret gap between the mountains," Lawson bragged as he jumped off the ATV, pleased with himself. "Time to walk."

"We can find a way around this."

"Sure, if ya climb. I ain't no climber," Lawson replied sternly, making it clear it wasn't up for negotiation. "Ya saddled up this pony, time to ride 'em cowboy."

What the fuck had Caelin gotten himself into? No man or grizzly in their right mind would get any closer to that deathtrap. Was this kind of suicidal madness the effect Daemiana had on males, like some siren enchanting them toward their demise?

"Giddyup."

"Y-Y-You *really* serious?"

"Ya catch on quick."

"That's m-m-more dangerous than having climbed over the mountains!"

"For you, maybe. Climb'in is in your blood. I can't climb worth a fuck."

No one had ever likened him to Dad that way. It felt good. But it changed nothing. And it was too late to go back. So, Caelin just glared at the seracs of the mildly steep glacier. *All to avoid a fucking climb*. Dad must have been turning in his grave.

Each treacherous step toward the death palace and into its ice cavern felt excruciatingly like his last. The white void succumbed to partial darkness beneath seracs which had merged enough to block out most of the sunlight.

"I don't kn-kn-know about this anymore," Caelin pleaded as he eyed the climbing rope linking his harness to Lawson's, who was yards ahead, pushing the ATV. More and more crevasses became discernible. That meant more and more crevasses were possibly indiscernible beneath the potentially thin ice at their feet.

If one of them were to be swallowed up, the plan was for the other to arrest the fall by hunkering into the ice with their ice axe until the line went taut, arresting the fall before both were dragged down to certain death. But with that fucking ATV—

"I ain't stupid, kid," Lawson grunted. "If I go under, I won't let the rig drag us down with it."

"I think I hear i-i-ice cracking..."

"SHHHHHHH!"

They stopped and remained quiet.

There was crunching and grinding overhead. Lawson scowled up at the serac as if it were being rude, then frantically hopped on the ATV and fired it up.

"Get on!"

"B-B-But that's too much weight per surface area—"

"Now!"

Caelin rushed the ATV, coiling the rope as he went, and jumped on as Lawson gunned it, barely evading the overhead serac's collapse. Lawson accelerated to full throttle, trying to outrun the other toppling seracs, one after the other like dominoes. The ice cavern was imploding. Tons of ice crashed down all around. The swooshing frost smacked and stung them like a subzero gale.

"Look out!"

"We're go'in straight, hell or high water, kid!"

They hit extrusions on the ice head-on, at full speed, one after the other like big speed bumps, thrusting them airborne, each higher and further than the last until—

They careened explosively out the opposite end of the crumbling ice palace and cartwheeled down a steep, snowy slope toward the interior, ATV and all.

They eventually came to rest on the soft powder.

Caelin stared up at the sky, dazed. Never again would he choose the low ground over the high ground; he vowed there and then. Dad had once said they were *highlanders*, that they were from a long line of mountain people and summiteers. Dad once fondly mentioned the summit of K2 as being the sweetest of all his adventures.

Caelin sat up and watched Lawson, already on his feet, yanking the ATV over, up onto its tires, looking more embarrassed than anything else. Caelin then staggered to his feet, knowing better than to say anything. He simply stared out at the no-man's-land ahead. The interior awaited them, intent on not being outdone by the death palace.

It was not long until they arrived at the lakeshore where Caelin had last seen Daemiana. Lawson's stunt had proven as fast or faster than going over the mountains. Maybe the scar-faced bear had used that crazy *shortcut* too, though a whole lot more gracefully, no doubt. Not that Caelin was tempted ever to try it again, faster or not.

They dismounted the ATV and looked around.

"This what we're look'in for, kid?" Lawson said, standing beside Daemiana's dried blood.

"They h-h-hurt her bad…"

"Killed her by the looks of it," Lawson lamented, appearing to regret having doubted her existence. "We'll make'em pay."

He grabbed the rifle strapped to his back and cocked it.

Caelin sighed, unwilling to accept her death.

Lawson began tracking by foot. It was for real now. The misadventures were over. The real mission had begun.

Caelin followed, pushing the ATV, determined to see it through to the end.

Late afternoon lurked as they delved deeper and deeper into the interior. It looked like nothing Caelin had ever seen. The dense forest canopy at times cast a strange, daytime darkness.

Nerves and a yearning to turn back set in. Maybe they had gone the wrong way—

Lawson gestured for Caelin to get down.

He did.

They listened.

Lawson began crawling the rest of the way.

Caelin did the same, leaving behind the ATV.

They arrived at a big river.

Something else gradually came into view near the opposite bank.

It was a small, rundown river cabin on rotting stilts. Daemiana was dangling from the adjacent gallows, over a pit, by her backwardly hyper-extended arms. Caelin gasped.

"They tortured and killed her!"

Lawson angrily gestured for Caelin to shut up. He did.

Daemiana's tangled hair eerily hung over her face. Her cloak was tightly wrapped around her body, from her chest to her ankles, with rope.

"Think they call this the Salmon River," Lawson casually muttered while glancing at his map.

"Wh-Wh-What?" Caelin whispered. Who cared about the river? What were they going to do?

"N' she's alive too," Lawson also casually mentioned.

"How do you know?"

"Been killing shit my whole life. I just know."

Caelin stared at him, at a loss for words.

"We'll rescue her first, then come back n' take care of these sick motherfucks," Lawson muttered cooly while glancing at his map again.

Miles upstream, they paralleled the river on the ATV, full speed, looking for somewhere to cross. They finally reached a fork where three shallower, fast-flowing rivers converged to form the main river. They then blew through the waist-deep shallows, full throttle, nearly rolling over the ATV before making it onto the other bank.

They then sped back downstream toward the river cabin.

Lawson killed the engine before the cabin became discernible in the distance. Caelin jumped off and helped him quietly push the ATV the rest of the way.

They meandered cautiously around an increasing number of bear traps as they neared the cabin and then hid. Caelin eyed the bear traps with intrigue while Lawson cased the place.

"Why so many traps?" Caelin whispered.

Lawson again gestured for him to shut up.

No one appeared to be guarding Daemiana.

They quietly rushed the gallows, pushing along the ATV, up to the edge of the deep, underlying pit. Lawson stood on the ATV, positioned his rifle at a steep, upward angle against the chain from which Daemiana was hanging. He looked down at Caelin, nodded, and pulled the trigger, blowing apart the chain.

Daemiana dropped a short fall onto Caelin's extended hands. He grabbed her and yanked her away from the pit, falling back with Daemiana in his arms. Lawson re-strapped his rifle to his back, pulled out his buck knife, cut the ropes binding her, placed her on the ATV, and jumped on. Caelin mounted the rig with Daemiana between he and Lawson and held her tight between his arms while clutching Lawson with all his might.

Lawson fired up the engine and gunned it as Beaudry, McConnolly, and Ivers were storming out of the cabin in disbelief.

Caelin couldn't help smiling with exhilaration as they escaped.

Beaudry furiously took aim with his rifle, but the ATV disappeared past the trees as he fired off a shot at one of the rear tires, which missed and ricocheted off a boulder.

Caelin jerked and screamed, nearly falling off the rig.

CHAPTER 19

Her body keeled off limply to the side as she was jolted awake by a panicked scream behind her. Daemiana's eyes opened to the sight of her tangled hair in her face. Dearest Mother... Her arms were too numb to lift. She grasped futilely at any sense of bearing—

"I'm sh-sh-shot!"

"What, goddamn it!? Where?!"

"I-I-I don't know!"

"Just hold on, kid!"

Was it that odious boy and another male?! Was she between them, atop a growling, mechanized beast? What was happening? Did not that boy intentionally get her captured back at the lake? Why then did it appear that he was rescuing her? She no longer knew what to believe as they accelerated faster and faster. Her hair began swaying like a willow in the wind, liberating her eyes. She flinched at the blur of wilderness streaking past them.

"I-I-I'm dying..." the boy moaned. "Mr. Lawson..."

Lawson glanced back at Caelin as he continued accelerating.

"You ain't dy'in, stupid! It just grazed ya!"

Daemiana glanced back at the boy as well. Blood was trickling from his nicked earlobe onto his shoulder—

"What the fuck?!" Lawson screamed as he skid the ATV to a stop.

Caelin slammed into Daemiana; both slammed into Lawson's back; all avoided falling off the rig.

"Well... That damn explains all them bear traps laid out all around the cabin," Lawson surmised.

The huge, anomalous grizzlies had them surrounded, foaming at the mouth, the fur on their backs raised.

"What's wrong with this damn picture?" Lawson pondered aloud. "That ain't natural bear behavior... They're in a pack, scared n' pissed, at the same time. But at what?"

Lawson whipped his head around and glared suspiciously at Caelin, then at Daemiana.

"Kid, what the fuck ain't ya tell'in me here?"

Daemiana could sense Signore Lawson's affinity to nature. He was deducing that which was inherently unnatural about the situation: *her*. Before she could flee, the boy screamed.

"They're charging!"

Lawson gunned the ATV. Daemiana gasped as the mechanized beast lurched forward and scarcely evaded the charging bears upon them: one, two, three at a time until it outran them all. She looked back in dismay. They had not only escaped the slayers but the beasts as well. She could not remember the last time males had defied her expectations with something other than betrayal.

She felt the boy's embrace tighten around her. Her heart pounded a little harder. She did not know why since she hated him. Fear, loathing, and distrust had never let her down. It made betrayal impossible. But at that moment, she could not remember the last time she felt safer, there in that odious boy's arms.

The ATV slowed to a stop at the Salmon River, miles upstream.

"Wh-Why'd we stop? Let's cross the way we came!"

"Kid," Lawson said while staring ahead pensively. "Ya gonna need more than just balls to survive out here."

"What? L-Let's go! Before the bears and the three psychos catch up—"

"Shut up," he ordered.

Daemiana had been right about Signore Lawson. He too felt Mother and all that was Hers. He too was feral. He too knew that something was on the opposite bank, in the riparian scrub, lying in wait; its big, furry shoulder hump nearly indiscernible as it protruded above the dense vegetation. But not to her, and not to Signore Lawson. They knew something was there—

It began advancing, faster and faster until it burst out of the scrub full speed and plowed through the shallows, eyes, and nostrils flaring. It was the scar-faced bear.

Lawson gunned the ATV, and off they sped, full throttle, away from the river.

"It's gaining fast!" Caelin cried.

Its hot, rancid grunts were closing in like deathly gales.

"He's gonna get m-m-me!"

Lawson swerved the rig as the scar-faced bear leapt and grazed Caelin's back with its claws.

"Ahhhhhhhhh! It got me!"

"Kid, if it'd a got ya, ya wouldn't still be here tell'in me about it!"

"Hurry!"

The bear was again gaining on them until they reached full speed, pulled away, and finally left it behind.

Lawson glanced back.

"If I didn't know better, I'd say it was personal with that disfigured son of a bitch!" Lawson pondered aloud and glanced back at Daemiana. "Biggest bear I ever seen! Any ideas about who or what fucked up its face like that?!"

She looked away

"N' why are those three fucks so hellbent after ya too?!"

Signore Lawson was piecing it all together. He glanced back at Daemiana a final time. She finally glared back.

"It seemed pretty goddamned personal with them too."

"We're going the wrong way!" Caelin lamented.

"Out here, kid, the only right way's survival!"

Signore Lawson's feral understanding of Mother's beasts, of the situation, and of her was a threat. Daemiana was more intent than ever on fleeing as soon as she was sure the beasts and the slayers were not near.

The ATV eventually groaned and smoked and slowed to a crawl as the wild grew denser, steeper, more rugged. It grew increasingly tangled in the shrubbery as its belly scraped over the underlying rocks of the increasingly hostile terrain.

"The rig's on its last legs," Lawson warned.

Eventually, it became stuck.

Lawson cranked the engine to full throttle, forcing it to smoke and grind and screech worse than ever.

"M-M-Maybe we should walk!"

"Ya think that fuck'in bear gave up on chase'in us?!" Lawson snapped. "Don't worry about the fuck'in rig! How about instead tell'in me why everyone and everything's so hot for your little girl-friend, here?!"

Signore Lawson no longer suspected that she was not natural. He *knew* it. If Signore Lawson came to fully understand what she was, would he also attempt to kill her? Like the Inquisitors? Like the beasts?

They lurched forward as the mechanized beast broke through the brush—

Lawson's eyes widened with horror. He leaned back, grabbed Caelin and Daemiana, and yanked them off the rig, down to the ground with him.

The ATV disappeared over a cliff ledge.

They all hit the ground, rolled, and went over as well.

"Dearest Mother!" Daemiana screamed.

If the boy had indeed rescued her from the Inquisitors, he was about to learn that risking oneself for another was a fool's errand. And that only Mother's Covenant, of survival of the fittest, lead to any true and lasting salvation.

CHAPTER 20

SHE GOUGED THE CLIFF FACE WITH HER NAILS. HER PLUMMET GRATED to a halt. Her fingers and toes ached from the tugging jolt. Rock was not as forgiving as flesh and bone. She clawed her way up and pounced high into the air, back onto the ledge. She instinctually fled.

The boy's terrified screams compelled her to stop.

Daemiana returned to the ledge against her better judgment. Signore Lawson was a threat. Like the scar-faced beast, like the Inquisitors, like Dionisio, like every male she had ever known. What if the boy proved no better? He had gotten her captured back at the lake. But then he rescued her.

She peered down. Caelin and Lawson were dangling from woody shrubs, which were slowly uprooting. The boy again screamed.

"Never scream like a bitch, boy!" fumed Lawson while glaring up at Daemiana.

"Take my hand," she reached for Caelin.

"I can't...r-r-reach..."

"Don't give that cooze your hand!" Lawson raged. "She ain't right!"

"I'm falling!" screamed the boy.

"Ain't natural how she jumped on outta here like a fuck'in cat!"

"Give me your hand!" Daemiana pleaded.

"It's why them fuck'in guys n' bears want her dead! She's evil!" Lawson ranted. "Bitches like her are like my ex-fuck'in-wives! Ya offer'em your heart, but they want your goddamned soul!"

Daemiana balked at Lawson's misogynistic vitriol. The foul brute knew nothing of her. He was the one who was not *right*!

The boy screamed as his woody shrub uprooted.

Daemiana sank her nails into the rock and lunged down as far as she could, thrusting her other claw into his forearm and arresting his fall. She yanked him up onto the ledge. The boy clutched his bleeding forearm. He was otherwise uninjured but stared at Daemiana, wide-eyed and mouth agape, in awe of her anomalous power.

Daemiana then looked down at Lawson, unsure what to do.

"Bitch, we know damn well I ain't take'in ya goddamned hand."

"Then you will die."

"The kid n' me died the moment we saved ya from what ya had come'in to ya."

Signore Lawson spewed his hate with chilling conviction.

"Had I known, I would'a killed ya myself," Lawson assured her.

"You know nothing, foul man—"

"Came to Alaska after my two ugly divorces to get away from bitches. But here we are. Even out here, ya cunts still did me in—"

Lawson's shrub uprooted, and he disappeared into the gulch. Daemiana closed her eyes, not wanting to see, yet she found herself sighing with relief that he was gone. She hated herself for it. When she opened her eyes, the boy was beside her, distraught at the sight of Lawson's mangled corpse on the jagged rocks far below, at a river's edge.

"Signore Lawson gambled wrong. He missed the water." she sighed, refusing to regret his death, as she undoubtedly would the boy's, if and when his time came. Signore Lawson despised females as much as she did males. What made her different than him, she was not sure, or willing to accept. The opposite of misogyny was misandry—

She spun around and gasped, moments before its rancid grunts were upon them. They were trapped.

"The bear!" screamed the boy.

The scar-faced bear had arrived snarling. It stood on its hind legs, towering 11-feet.

"Despair not. He wants only me," she assured the boy, who was still reeling from Lawson's death.

Daemiana charged the wicked beast with superhuman speed and clawed at its belly. But it wrapped her with its monstrous forelegs and bore down on her with its 3000-pound bear hug, crushing her down to the ground and locking its mammoth jaws on her head.

Its putrid drool sloshed into her nose and mouth as it mauled her, making her writhe and scream more than from the pain—

The bear whimpered suddenly. It leapt off her.

The boy had stabbed its hump with his dagger.

The bear roared with a fiery rage.

Caelin backed away, clutching his dagger, turning pale.

The bear again locked its jaws on Daemiana's head, then thrashed her around like a limp salmon and thrust her away from the ledge to ensure no escape. She hit the ground hard and winced in agony, no match for it. Mother's beasts ruled the daytime.

Daemiana staggered to her feet, bleeding profusely.

Other bears were arriving.

She was trapped and surrounded. The scar-faced bear stood between her and the ledge. Daemiana backed away as the scar-faced bear pounced at her. She dodged its ferocious claw strikes while gaging her speed advantage.

It charged.

She hopped onto its head — barely evading its jaws — and ran across its back, then jumped back toward the ledge.

"We must leap to escape!" she told Caelin.

"W-W-What...?" the boy stammered with dread, looking at her as if she were insane.

She took his hand, unwilling to jump without him. He'd again fought to protect her when he stabbed the bear. Perhaps, he was not so odious. But would he survive her, assuming he survived the jump?

The boy forced himself to put on a brave face for her. He nodded.

Together they sprinted and jumped off the ledge as far as they could, barely evading the scar-faced bear's last incensed claw strike.

CHAPTER 21

THEY PLUMMETED 100-FEET AND SMASHED INTO THE RIVER'S FROTHY turbulence. They missed the rocks but not the impact's fiery sting. They were swept away. A heinous cold writhed Caelin to his core. He choked down water as he flailed against the downward tow of his gear and armored coat. He succumbed to the thought of drowning over the protracted death that abandoning his gear so deep in the interior would surely inflict.

His pent desperation burst, overcoming the stun of the frigid whitewater. Caelin kicked and paddled until his air-starved mouth broke the water surface like a blowhole, spewing mist as he gasped and wretched. The water and air were then busted out of his lungs as he slammed into the rocky bank of the narrowing rapids. He hugged the jagged boulder, which both saved and nearly killed him. Caelin fought for each breath.

He crawled out of the river eventually. He was intact, gear and all. A final coughing fit gouged the lingering water from his lungs. He rolled onto his back and winced as he clutched his battered ribs.

Daemiana was standing over him, draped in her soaking cloak, unfazed by it all. The haunting sight reminded him of her awesome yet unnatural power. And why Lawson, the scar-faced bear, and the slayers were so appalled by her. Unlike them, though, Caelin was not. He smiled with relief they both survived.

His smile was unreciprocated. They had escaped and survived, but instead of looking happy, she seemed to be frowning at him. Was the prospect of ever understanding her hopeless?

"You made a grave mistake returning for me," she said.

What? Where was her gratitude? He and Lawson had just saved her. Lawson died doing so!

Caelin struggled to sit up.

"You are unable to help me because you cannot protect yourself from me," Daemiana warned.

What was she getting at?! Did she want his help or not?! Caelin furiously jumped to his feet, but the surge of anger was dispatched by shooting pain. He keeled over, clutching his ribs.

"Now, you tell me! Whatever the hell that m-m-means," Caelin lamented.

The gravity in her eyes was nothing short of deadly. She was not acting coy. The boy-girl games were over.

"What's changed between now and the other day?" Caelin demanded to know.

"I am beginning to care what happens to you."

Caelin finally looked at her. Her eyes were filled with genuine concern for him, "Flee for your life. Darkness is upon us. It may be already too late."

Only then did it click in Caelin's racked mind as he realized the light of day was waning. He *had* fucked up. He'd failed to consider what he'd do *after* rescuing her.

"I shall follow your scent all night and kill you. Unless you get far enough away."

Caelin remembered the Inquisitors' pit. Is that what it was for, to trap Daemiana in at night somehow? And to Lawson's point, had it really been Daemiana who had disfigured the giant bear?

"Flee or die, foolish boy!" she yelled. "Now!"

Caelin was smacked back into the moment. Run, but where to? Caelin hobbled away hurriedly along the riverbank. This wasn't how it was supposed to end, with him fleeing like a feckless weakling before she killed him. He felt as humiliated as he was terrified.

"Faster!" she screamed as she bolted away in the opposite direction, presumably to give him as much of a headstart as possible.

Caelin's mind raced as he stumbled along, searching for an inkling of what to do next. No solution existed, not one where he saw himself surviving the night. He remembered all too vividly his first night in the interior. He had survived Daemiana by sheer luck. His thoughts inevitably circled back to all he knew. What would Dad do?

"The current can be your best friend or your worst enemy," Caelin remembered Dad saying on a backpacking trip once, after a juvenile moose blew by and leaped into a river. It was swept away and devoured by the rapids.

"Sometimes both," Dad continued as the pursuing grizzly stopped at the water's edge, giving up the chase. The moose had escaped the bear, but had it survived rapids? No time to worry about it.

Caelin jumped back into the river before he could stop himself and was again scourged by the cold and rocky whitewater. It soon felt like he was blowing through a fire hydrant. The bed and bank began resembling a chute. The rocks were a blur. The turbulence became like a suffocating foam. The intensifying acceleration made death the only certainty. A misty roar was upon him. It meant one thing. It was closer than he had hoped. He had gambled wrong.

Caelin screamed as he tumbled over a waterfall and plunged toward a white abyss. He ripped into the heart of a raging eddy, which thrashed him head-over-heels for what felt like an eternity, showing no intent of letting him go. But it finally did, seconds before he lost consciousness.

Caelin crawled out of the water's mauling cold, shivering, teeth chattering. He collapsed. His eyes slowly closed. Just for a little bit. Only for a moment. To rest. A little while longer.

"Never close your eyes when hypothermic," Dad would say. "Or you're dead."

Caelin forced his eyes to open before drifting into shock and eventual death. He resumed crawling, weighed down by his soaked clothes, armored coat, pack, and gear. While it was a miracle, he had not lost any of it yet; it was all useless to him at that moment.

His shivering bordered on seizures as he stacked wood circularly to build a fire. He struggled to find and yank the waterproof matches out from his pant pocket but finally managed. But they wouldn't light. They wouldn't fucking light!

"Sh-Sh-Shit!"

That was it... He was going to die...

It was why Dad never relied on matches.

So Caelin frantically undid and removed a shoelace, the way Dad would. He coiled it around a long, smooth, robust twig — as tightly as he could.

He pressed the twig's tip down, perpendicularly, on a strip of dry bark and tugged desperately at both ends of the shoelace, rotating the twig's tip back and forth against the bark, faster and faster and faster, until smoke began to rise. Caelin let out a relieved sob. He tugged at the shoelace harder and harder, resenting himself for hating Dad's stern survivalist training. It was about to save his life.

The bark eventually caught fire.

A rowdy bonfire bobbed and weaved and jabbed at him.

He relished its infernal heat while he dried his clothes over it.

A blood-curdling howl boomed in the distance.

Caelin looked up.

The nearly full moon overhead warned that it'd be worse than last time if he didn't figure something out.

After frantically dressing, he hurriedly kicked aside and stomped some of the fire's smoking ash to cool it. He then lathered the ash all over his clothes, boots, pack, and himself.

"You can't have prey or predator smell you coming," Dad preached at the dawn of every hunt while lathering himself in ash like it were some sacred ritual.

Caelin then frenziedly kicked and tossed much of the bonfire's burning wood in all directions — creating small, scattered fires all around — to further mask his scent.

He grabbed his gear and fled as macabre growls rapidly neared.

Caelin ran up on the biggest tree.

He tossed his pack to the ground, pulled out a climbing rope, attached one end to the pack, the other to his harness.

He took a deep breath, rubbed his quivering hands together to quell them, then climbed calmly and steadily. No missteps.

Caelin ascended high up the tree, deep into its dense foliage, and hoisted up his gear with the rope. He remained desperately still as—

The werewolf emerged below.

Its crimson cloak dangled down its back.

It circled the area, glaring at the rowdy, jabbing fires, sniffing insatiably, over and over, like a predator closing in on stealthy prey.

It circled and circled, then disappeared, only to reemerge and circle again, over and over, with a floaty, anomalous swiftness and silence.

Sitting high up the tree, hidden, Caelin was clutching the trunk tightly with one arm and his gear with the other. His own silence was his only hope for survival. He eventually mustered the will to glance down.

She was huge, monstrous. With the fuller moon, she was fuller beast. Daemiana was no longer there. All Caelin saw was a hideous, canid abomination.

It let out a booming howl that pierced his ears.

He closed his eyes, laboring to keep calm and quiet.

It resumed circling as if trying to break him and cause him to slip up and reveal his location.

Caelin's arms ached from exhaustion, though he dared not move. Or it'd be over. The slayers and scar-faced bear were not around to save him like last time. So Caelin bit his lip, fighting through the agony as the werewolf's virulent evil was withering his heart, eroding his will, and sapping his soul. Death had finally had cornered him.

He held his breath, more than ever regretting the journey and having never felt more alone. Ivers had been right. There was nothing Caelin could do to help her. He wasn't strong enough, as Ivers had warned.

He was no hero; he finally accepted that.

He should have heeded the ample warnings.

All he could hope for now was a swift, painless death.

CHAPTER 22

A TONGUE FLICKED HIS CHAPPED LIPS, MOISTENING THEM WITH EACH soft, sweet dab. He let it nestle deep in his mouth. Nothing was like her delicious warmth. He opened his eyes, wanting more. The werewolf was there in the tree with him, snout to mouth.

Caelin recoiled and fell.

He awakened — realizing he'd dozed off — as he crashed down onto a lower limb, unable to hold on, and continued falling and crashing into lower limbs until he managed to grasp one and arrest his fall, before again losing his grip and plummeting into lower limbs, one after the other, over and over; his battered ribs bearing the brunt of most every blow and pine needle sting.

He smashed into the ground feet-first, ass-second.

The agony screeched up his spine and out his mouth before he could muffle it with his hands. He lay back and writhed quietly till the pain let up enough for him to think straight. He was a sitting duck for the werewolf. But it was nowhere to be seen. All he saw was his gear, which had landed nearby.

Caelin scrambled to it, grabbed it, dashed back to the tree. He hunkered beside it, bracing for anything. The bluish predawn grim was as menacing as anything he had seen. His fires were nothing but ghostly pale plumes. The moon was fading. A light mist had crept in. He began climbing back up the tree when he noticed nearby: feminine contours slowly reveling in the haze, swaying about gracefully. The playful flaps of her cloak teased him with fleeting glimpses as she danced. Her return soothed him. It drew him without hesitation. His eyes preened every dewy curve of her slender form as he neared. He wanted her there and then as he reached for her.

Daemiana slowed and collapsed before he could lustfully take her into his arms. She suddenly went from svelte to hulking werewolf and pounced on him. She was about to devour him, but the dwindling predawn blue succumbed to the glow of dawn. Daemiana collapsed again, down onto him, again in human form, asleep.

Caelin lay there, beneath her, too shocked to react, too stunned by the fluid swiftness of her duality.

"Stupid mistakes will kill you faster than a fucking bullet," Dad constantly warned. What had Caelin been thinking? That stupid mistake had nearly gotten him killed just then. After the great lengths he'd taken to survive the night, just to throw it all away in a moment of reckless disregard for the fact that Daemiana was not herself at night.

Caelin gently rolled her off him.

He sat up and stared out at the distance in stoic silence, numb.

Daemiana eventually awoke and curled into a ball, her back to him. The longsome quiet eventually broke.

"You are alive."

Her tone was one of cold indifference.

"Flee. Before it is again night. Go far, far away."

Caelin ever so slightly, yet adamantly, shook his head: no. Things were different now. There was a defiant pride kindling in him. It felt alien, yet it felt real, and it felt right. He had survived the impossible by his own volition. He was beginning to believe in himself, maybe for the first time in his life.

"I'll be alright."

"Do not be foolish."

Foolish? He manned up and survived! Most anyone else would have died. But not him. She couldn't take that away. No one could. It was his. Forever.

"You can go, knowing that you helped me escape the Inquisitors," she persisted.

"The only way to fix this is to find a cure."

"You will not survive another night."

"I can take care of myself."

"Just go."

He refused.

"I cannot give you what you want," she finally said.

"What I want?"

She would not turn to face him.

"What if other knights have sought to help me? Long before you."

Other knights? Caelin was unsure he heard right.

"What if they all failed?"

"You think I'm a knight?" Caelin said, his ego swelling.

"What if they all died trying?"

Caelin looked down; his bubble burst too quickly.

"Do you still desire to help me?"

Caelin still relished the thought of being her knight. The Inquisitor dagger was his sword and the coat his armor.

"Or, do you now wish to go?"

"There's nothing for me to go back to."

"I cannot give you what you want, nor can I replace all you have lost. I cannot help you honor the memory of your dead father. I cannot mend your heart."

Caelin nodded with solemn acceptance. It was what it was. Not that a happy ending was ever in the cards for him. Not in this shit life. Maybe in the next. It was something he'd long accepted. He was

— as he had been for some time — stockpiling good Karma. Just doing the best he could, as best he knew.

"I know," he sighed, but he knew nothing. He was still so hot for her, even after everything that'd happened. Caelin had to get it together and refocus—

Daemiana sat up and drew closer. They locked eyes.

"I am beginning to care more and more whether or not you die, knight," she whispered and sealed it with a kiss.

He had given up trying to understand her. But there it was, her final warning to him. Only he wasn't hearing it. He just wanted her no matter what, at any cost as he glimpsed her breasts through the opening in her cloak. He instead grabbed her neck, pulled her closer, gently nuzzled his thumb on her jugular cleft, then penetrated her mouth ravenously with his tongue. That was his warning to her, sealed too with a kiss. He was capable of devouring her as well. And, he was the only man who could save her because he was capable of anything for her.

CHAPTER 23

His passions were only escalating. He knew no restraint. She had told him she could not give him what he wanted. It was happening so fast. His torrent of lust forayed and engulfed her. It devolved into nothing short of vulgar. His fervid hands slipped inside her cloak as his tongue fucked her mouth. He *was* different. The taste of fear was gone from him. She pushed away his mucky passions, stood, and backed away, no longer in control. He had taken that away. It scared her. It angered her. The gall, the insolence...

He again neared, undeterred, unapologetic, bent on resuming what he began. Something fiery in him had been awoken, something that should not have been, something from which nothing good could come, something seeking what she could not give him. It had never been her intention for it all to come this far. He should have died or fled after having served his purpose!

He again grabbed her and resumed ravishing her. She pondered, ripping out his throat or tearing into his heart if only to make him stop. After all, he had served his purpose. She was free of the Inquisitors and the beasts. If she fled and disappeared into Mother's bosom, never looking back, neither he nor any of the other pursuing males would ever find her. She would be free to find another way in another land. She would be free to make her own way—

Her knees went weak. A salacious sigh emanated from her lips. Her eyes closed. His sultry mouth was licking its way down her neck like fevered waves lapping netherly. Before she knew, it was sullying her left breast so ravenously, the nipple tendered and throbbed with exult.

His hands were oozing like honey down her back — lower and lower — until they grabbed, squeezed, and spread her ass cheeks.

She gasped and slapped away his hands; another potentially sweet and tender moment again killed by his barbarity. Before she could flee, he was already crouched and animally slobbering down her navel while his hands gushed up her thighs like magma. His tongue and fingers seemed intent on rendezvousing somewhere between her legs.

She slapped away his mouth before it could lay further siege and shoved him. He flew back and hit the ground hard, rolling to a rest, face-up and dazed. His strength was no match. She would never cede control. And that was his final warning.

He seemed oblivious to the nonverbal. It was as if a lifetime of pent lust had finally erupted. And yet...

She found herself approaching him rather than fleeing. His vilely yearnings had them careening toward nothing good, and still, she found herself straddling him before she could stop herself, back in control, needing at least that. She lowered her mouth to his to let him resume kissing her while she gently nipped at his tongue with her teeth to subdue it before it again ran rampant in her mouth and overwhelmed her better judgment. She battled to tame his male will until he kissed and held her in a manner she so yearned. It did not last.

He had undone his pants somehow, and his ever swelling phallus pulsed hard against her lower back. She clenched his scrotum and squeezed to reassert control. That dark triad made males hopeless. It poisoned the carnal and the spiritual, sowing as much death as new life, racking all fems between madonna and whore. It knew no middle, no moderation, no mercy; neither Father, nor Son, nor Holy Spook. Males were self-serving hypocrites. And that was why she hated them—

His tongue had again gone rampant in her mouth while his fervid hands squeezed her derriere. His nefarious phallus throbbed harder and harder against her. His savagery was again overwhelming her. She finally grabbed the phallus itself to subdue it. He grunted like a brute with every tug, his eyes fixed on her breasts' every bounce, his teeth clenched, his brow wrinkled and beaded with sweat, his muscles tightening and tightening, his groans eventually bellowing to a euphoric crescendo as he jerked and writhed and spewed hot goo all over her arm and back with each spasm of his phallus until it limped and receded into catharsis, as did the rest of him.

She rested her head on his chest and closed her eyes. That was the best she could do for him. What she had to do to be held in silence. She listened to his heart slow, and she finally got what she wanted. He held her for a long while. Perhaps his evil male will could be tamed so that he would not let her down like every male before him.

Just then—

Her skin crawled.

Her nerves grated to a dull burn.

Her mind whorled with morbid visions.

A darkness clenched her heart.

Mother became deathly silent.

Birds, deer, insects were fleeing past them.

It meant only one thing: *they* had arrived.

She jumped to her feet and fled in the same direction as Mother's creatures.

Caelin sat up, perplexed.

"What's the matter?"

Daemiana had again instinctually fled without him. She had to stop doing that, especially since it was now evident he had not yet served his entire purpose. She again needed him. So, Daemiana stopped and turned.

"This way! We must go! At once! Run!"

It was his final test. If they miraculously survived the coming onslaught, that would make him her longest surviving knight in shining armor; perhaps even making him *the one* who could save her from the accurst existence she was fleeing. Perhaps he was the one male who would never let her down, the one she could finally trust and truly believe in always.

CHAPTER 24

Birds whisked overhead. A fox blew out of its den. Deer dashed by. Woodrats scurried. Bugs zipped past him. Nature was fleeing like hell itself were in pursuit. Even after decades in the gray, on the hunt, joy deferred, dreams forsaken, all for a greater good, in a better place... It had not grown easier stomaching a fight against that which killed every one of his contemporaries: the Coven. Daemiana's kind had arrived to rescue her, as Ivers had feared. Time had run out.

Ivers drew his sword and charged the unseen macabre being fled by nature. Beaudry and McConnolly would know to do the same. But having split up to flank Daemiana had possibly sealed their demises against the coming onslaught. All that terrified Ivers at that moment was dying before all could be made right. Faith alone had long proven cheap. His reverberant regrets ached more than his worn innards and aged bone.

The distance was long. Every stride racked his knees and scathed his lungs. He was sputtering like an old engine. Running was fast becoming an impossibility while the dread of failure fueling him no longer proved enough. He stumbled and slowed to a brisk hobble, to avoid all-out collapse. He was too spent to fight and had no choice but to stop and catch his breath.

Ivers struggled to listen over his heaving wheezes and pommeling heart. Something was coming at him from beyond the shrubs and conifers, he finally realized. It sounded too small to be a moose. It was not as deft as a deer. It wasn't a bear. Dear God...

Ivers hid behind a tree and waited until the impeccably last moment to recommit to the mission, rather than succumbing to the fatigue imploring him to end it all with an ambush kill maneuver, his specialty.

But at the last second, the doubts again resurfaced and lingered. Perhaps he'd done all he could, in the best of faith, like McConnolly had raged too many times. The Order was allowed to abort a mission when it began bordering on suicide and slay as viciously as needed to retreat and escape. The rule was too often abused, though, and he long vowed never again. Since then, he struggled to discern when it was time to persevere or retreat. It was why Ivers had dragged out this mission, his last mission, for far too long. Or perhaps it was due to his self-serving quest for redemption, as McConnolly had once implied. Was not Ivers, therefore, legitimately justified in finally ending it there and then?

No. He had an obligation to do the right thing, no matter how difficult. The mission had to be seen through to the end. If it perfectly aligned with his self-serving need for redemption, so be it.

It was time.

Instead of executing a kill maneuver, Ivers holstered his sword and pounced, wrapped, and tackled the feral darling as she and the boy dashed by. He handcuffed one of her wrists before she tossed him off with her abominable strength and pounced back to her feet. But Ivers held on to the opposite cuff and yanked her back toward him. Ivers again wrapped her with both arms, then thrust her high into the air and suplexed her head so viciously into the ground, her neck snapped. Ivers then pounced on her as she lay on the ground facefirst, paralyzed, at least for a while. It would not be long before the injury fully healed, and she would try to kill him. The neck-break maneuver was Ivers' age-old means of immobilizing abominables, nonlethally; developed and perfected by him decades ago.

Ivers then yanked Daemiana's arms behind her back and cuffed the second wrist just as the boy pounced onto his back to stop him. Ivers pried apart Caelin's arms and tossed him up and over his shoulder. Caelin face-planted on the ground.

Ivers stumbled back, gasping for air, more agonized and exhausted than ever. It took everything in him not to collapse. His lethality, unlike the rest of him, fortunately, had not deteriorated as much in his old age.

"We will all die!" the girl screamed in terror. "Release us! We can all flee together!"

Ivers instead hogtied her by shackling and jerking back her ankles and then fastening the shackles to the handcuffs.

"They are here!" she screamed.

That, Ivers knew. Why she was so terrified, he did not know. After all, they were here to rescue her. It was he and the boy who would likely soon be dead.

"They will kill us all!"

Ivers' hair swayed as something red streaked past him.

He turned and felt it dash behind him.

Ivers drew his sword, pulled the hood of his armored coat over his head, and assumed a high guard defense.

"Stay down, boy!" Ivers warned as Caelin stumbled about, trying to stand.

For death was cloaked in crimson, not black. It was converging and circling them with abominable speed. The Coven — Daemiana's coven — had arrived. Dionisio, LeVee, Mikaela, Cybilia, and Demetria.

Ivers' mind was forever gashed with their memory. Those diabolically black eyes, those canid noses and teeth. That rust-tinged hue to their inhumanly tight, pale skin. Those lanky, clawed limbs. They towered nearly seven feet, nude and barefoot beneath their crimson cloaks and void of any remnant traces of humanity even in their daytime form — unlike Daemiana, who had undergone weeks of spiritual treatment by Ivers at the river cabin before her escape to Kreuger Sound. That was why she was nearly human in her daytime, non-werewolf form as a result, rather than remaining stuck as some daytime in-between thing. While the curse could not be broken, it could be weakened, at least during the day.

"Grand Inquisitor. Have we not learned to live in peace? After so much bloodshed," lamented the alpha werewolf, Dionisio, in a hideous guttural rumble. He was the biggest and most menacing. "After centuries in Siberia, feeding only on animals, harming no one, the Church continues to hunt us. The Church continues to desire war!"

"Cause you n' your kind ain't right!" McConnolly flanked them as Beaudry tore into their opposite flank.

Ivers charged the Coven head-on, completing the triangulation.

"Then death, you shall all have!" Dionisio roared.

The Coven pounced like cats in all directions over the slayers' sword strikes.

Ivers lost sight of Dionisio in the chaos, who had charged after Daemiana.

Ivers turned and charged after him.

The boy drew his dagger and stood guard over the girl but was no match. Dionisio clawed him and sent him flying back. Dionisio then yanked up the helpless, hogtied girl by the hair, tore into her throat with his claws, and began trying to tear off her head while she screamed.

"NO!" Ivers frantically opened fire at Dionisio with his gun to save the girl, not understanding why the Coven wanted to kill her; she was one of them. Why were they not trying to rescue her? Not that it mattered. Losing the girl, whether by the Coven rescuing or killing her, was unacceptable. The spiritual treatment and bloodshed would have all been in vain!

Ivers emptied the clip into Dionisio's head as he desperately closed in on him, only stunning him. The girl had to live long enough for Ivers to break and ritually kill her himself to break the curse, which was not only gripping her but the entire Coven as well. Or so, Ivers theorized. The Coven had likely entered into the cursed pact as a group, not individually. Thus, ritually breaking the curse in one would eradicate the curse in them all.

Ivers thrust his sword at Dionisio as he rushed him.

Dionisio let go of Daemiana and somersaulted over Ivers' swooshing blade, landing behind him. Ivers spun around and grazed Dionisio's chest with a spinning counterstrike. Ivers then lunged forward and thrust his sword at Dionisio's heart, but again Dionisio somersaulted over him. Ivers again spun around and narrowly missed Dionisio's throat with his blade.

LeVee and Zemetria tore into Beaudry.

Mikaela tore into McConnolly.

The slayers counterstruck and deflected the Coven's blur of claws and teeth.

McConnolly ducked a claw to the face and thrust his sword into Mikaela's stomach, to a loud searing hiss, not before she grazed his throat with her other claw. Both fell to the ground, McConnolly clutching his bleeding throat and Mikaela shrieking in agony.

Mikaela scurried onto McConnolly and tried to maul his face. McConnolly shielded himself with one arm and drew his gun with the opposite hand. He jammed the barrel into her jaws and fired every round into her mouth. She fled on all fours, wailing.

Beaudry evaded the onslaught of LeVee's and Zemetria's claws by bobbing and dodging and blocking and jumping back and lunging forward and diving to the ground and rolling back onto his feet, with stunning ease, speed, and prowess as if lulling in some exquisitely perfect moment.

Beaudry countered via a crouching, backspin sword strike to Zemetria's stomach, disemboweling her and then beheading her with a seamless, frontal spinning leap-strike to the throat, with the opposite hand, all in a single fluid motion.

Zemetria's head rolled along the ground spewing blood and deafening shrieks. Her body thrashed and contorted, gushing steaming blood until eventually dying.

The Coven retreated and disappeared into the wild as quickly as they arrived.

Daemiana broke through the handcuffs in desperation, fully healed. She clawed at her shackles. Beaudry re-holstered his sword and pounced on her. Before he could re-handcuff her, she clawed his face. Beaudry drew and smashed the butt of his dagger into her forehead, knocking her out. He then stood, yanked her up by the hair, and pressed the blade against her throat, drawing blood, about to cut off her head. He was still locked in the throes of combat—

"Beaudry!" Ivers growled, trying to make him settle down.

"Do it..." McConnolly groaned, clutching his own bleeding throat. "How many more have to die?"

"Stand down!" Ivers raged at Beaudry while tending to McConnolly's throat. He doused the wound with peroxide.

McConnolly screamed in agony while Ivers stitched him up. "Leave her be, Beaudry! NOW!" Ivers again growled.

But Beaudry remained bent on blood. His eyes were incensed, and his forehead vein was bulging. He looked as intent on killing Daemiana as Dionisio had. His piety had succumbed to wrath. His veneer of discipline and self-control was gone.

"Watch out!" Ivers yelled.

Beaudry ducked Caelin's ice axe swing to the back of his head, then spun around and smashed the butt of his dagger into Caelin's back. Caelin and Daemiana both fell at his feet. Beaudry slammed his foot down on Daemiana's back, holstered his dagger, unholstered his sword, and pressed it against Daemiana's neck.

"Beaudry! Stand down!" Ivers fumed. "That's an order!"

It was all coming close to unraveling.

Daemiana roused from unconsciousness.

Caelin's eyes locked on hers. Her eyes were welling up with tears. The sight of the blood and tears streaming down her face made something snap in him. The rage smoldering in Caelin's eyes began rivaling Beaudry's.

Caelin suddenly grabbed and yanked the gun from Beaudry's ankle holster, aimed it up at him, and stumbled back to his feet.

Beaudry just glared back at him unflinchingly.

"Thus saith the Lord: Behold I will judge thy cause, and will take VENGEANCE for thee."

"Unless you're God, asshole, better focus on the nice parts of the Bible," Caelin replied, shifting his aim from Beaudry's heart to Beaudry's face, with no hesitation.

Ivers tightened, unable to believe his eyes.

Had the boy finally crossed that wide, gray line into manhood? From which there'd be no going back and no more mercy shown. Caelin had become as much of a threat to the mission as the Coven.

CHAPTER 25

Beaudry re-handcuffed and re-hogtied Daemiana while glaring at Caelin, daring him to shoot. And shoot Caelin finally did, missing, lacking proficiency with the weapon.

"Goddamn, you both!" Ivers exploded. "Stop!" Instead—

Caelin retook aim at Beaudry's face, his eyes promising not to miss again. All control of the mission had been lost. Ivers' growing irrelevancy and invisibility anguished him. It was like he were already dead. Old age did that to people, but Ivers never imagined it finally happening during a mission. He felt powerless to control anything anymore, except his decision to resume stitching McConnolly's throat and try to stop the bleeding.

Beaudry wisely backed away from Daemiana, though he and Caelin still looked intent on killing each other. Beaudry, the most pious and disciplined of them all, had gone uncharacteristically unhinged at the same time the boy had chosen to grow a pair of balls.

"I'll kill you all!" Caelin screamed.

The boy's newfound will to kill was a grave passage rite that had thrust him into the burdens and lethalities of manhood, for which there could be no going back, for which there could be no clemency.

"Continue backing toward me," Ivers told Beaudry. "No sudden moves—"

"Kill the bitch!" McConnolly demanded, re-escalating the situation.

"I'll fucking kill all you guys!" Caelin screamed back. "Fuck you!"

"Everyone, shut up!" Ivers yelled over all of them.

"Kill the bitch and end this before we all die tonight at their fuck'in jaws!" McConnolly ranted.

"Take over patching up McConnolly!" Ivers ordered Beaudry, who was still backing up, drawing closer.

Ivers' failed leadership had led them there. He began longing for the days when no one dared cross him. Days put long behind him, by the grace of God. Days when he was as lethal as Beaudry, as defiant as McConnolly, as obsessed with the wrong girl as Caelin, and more fervently self-righteous than all of them.

"Kill her!" McConnolly raged.

Ivers furiously stopped stitching and clamped both hands tightly around McConnolly's throat. The extremes had been the vice of Ivers' youth, where he dwelled and ruled, commanding only fear and respect. He'd been wrong to let it all fade with age.

McConnolly blued, unable to breathe.

"The mission will not be aborted. Not now, not ever," Ivers rasped into McConnolly's ear.

McConnolly finally conceded a nod.

Ivers let go.

McConnolly coughed and gagged violently.

Ivers stood and glared into Beaudry's pale, stoic eyes.

"Flank the punk," Ivers whispered menacingly. "After you finish patching up this turd."

Beaudry took over, stitching McConnolly's throat.

Ivers approached Caelin slowly, hands up, his eyes subtly looking for the right moment and means to kill him. If Caelin didn't kill Ivers first. The trembly gun barrel aimed at Ivers' face had him a deafening flash from eternity.

"We're out of time. The full moon is upon us."

"Shut up!" Caelin replied.

Ivers pointed at Zemetria's beheaded corpse and decided to be blunt. Nothing would be more shocking and distracting than the truth.

"By merely killing her, we have sent her soul to hell—"

"I don't give a fuck!" Caelin fumed.

"The Coven are all locked together in a cursed pact with Satan."

"I don't believe in that shit! Step the fuck back!"

Ivers then pointed at Daemiana.

"If we can break just one of them through repentance and ritual Romanum Execution, we can break the entire Coven's cursed pact and emancipate them all! Possibly even saving ALL their souls, including the ones already in hell, God willing! I must do this! I must do it, NOW!"

"She's not one of them! She's nothing like them!"

"ONLY because of the spiritual treatment I administered. It weakened the curse in her."

"You were torturing her! You were readying to kill her!"

Ivers' hand was subtly inching toward his gun.

"Beneath tonight's full moon, they will all fully shift—"

"You're not gonna convince me to let you kill her!"

"She alone killed most of my men last full moon before escaping!" Ivers warned. "With four other werewolves out there, make no mistake, no one will be spared, not you, not your town, no one! The cursed pact must be broken, and it must be broken now!"

Caelin was still unfazed.

Ivers had no choice. He was going to have to reveal the most shocking truth of all in hopes of distracting Caelin enough to get off a headshot and end the standoff.

"If you continue down this path, you will one day have to make things right. By killing her yourself."

A nerve had finally been struck.

"Wh-What?" Caelin replied.

"I never told anyone this..." Ivers sighed. "I wasn't much older than you when it happened."

It had to finally be said. To let it be known. It was Ivers' darkest secret.

"Isabella was the first one I ever captured alive. When I was a young slayer, hunting alone. Isabella was one of them. But something went wrong during the spiritual treatment. I lost my focus. I came to love her."

"You traitorous son of a bitch!" McConnolly exploded, clearly hearing it for the first time. "I knew your sympathies for'em were rooted in no fucking good!"

"You are why our beloved Isabella vanished?!" Daemiana cried, coming to know it for the first time as well.

No one had noticed Beaudry slip away during the commotion.

"I murdered Isabella in a fit of anger," Ivers warned Caelin. "When it became clear that she was unattainable; a feral darling who could never love me back. Oh, I still fantasize about happy endings... About a normal life with Isabella. Instead, she burns in hell because of me, because of my selfish failure to her and to the mission."

"No—"

"ALL we can do for them is save their souls from eternal hellfire."

"You're wrong, you sick fuck," Caelin replied.

Ivers furiously drew his gun to kill him as—

Beaudry flanked Caelin from behind, grabbing, yanking up, and backwardly hyper-extending his arm, forcing Caelin to drop the gun before getting off a shot. Beaudry then foot-swept Caelin's legs from under him, slamming him down to the ground and viciously pummeling his face with hammer punches until he went limp.

Ivers stood over and locked eyes with Caelin, who was drifting in and out of consciousness. His nose was bubbling blood, his eyes were streaming teary rage.

"Fuck you..." Caelin mumbled.

It had taken Ivers decades to capture another one alive in order to make everything right. Nothing was going to stop him from breaking and ritually killing, Daemiana. To finally shatter that Goddamned curse.

"Execute him," Ivers ordered with no hesitation, his regression to ruthless sociopath complete. "For we are justified by Faith Alone."

"No!" Daemiana cried as Ivers dragged her away.

Beaudry kicked Caelin into unconsciousness.

Any remnants of mercy and compassion were gone from Ivers' eyes.

CHAPTER 26

His head bounced with every rock, bump and hollow, as his body grated along the ground. He roused and pulled focus on the jostling trees overhead. His eyes eventually fixed on someone's massive back. His ankles were tucked beneath a huge arm. He was being dragged away by Beaudry. Caelin twisted, turned, and tried to kick himself free. He hooked an arm around a passing tree.

Beaudry turned and kicked him in the gut till he let go. He then tightened his grip around Caelin's ankles using both hands, spun him around violently, and thrust him into a nearby gully. Caelin tumbled down the steep slope and slammed face-first into a frigid stream. His lips and teeth busted on the rocky bed. A plume of red bloomed and thinned and faded into the drift as the steely taste of blood filled his mouth.

Beaudry grabbed Caelin's hair, submerged his head, held him underwater.

"Repent ye, and be baptized," Beaudry preached as Caelin flailed futilely. Beaudry then yanked Caelin up before he drowned, thrust him up into the air, and expertly slammed him down to the ground, headfirst, away from the stream. Caelin bounced to a rest facedown, with Beaudry on top of him. Beaudry sealed Caelin's mouth with his hand and Caelin's ear with his hot, sweaty mouth.

"Thou shalt not copulate with any beast. Whosoever copulateth with a beast, shall be put to death."

Caelin's muffled screams reached a fever pitch.

"He that shall copulate with any beast, dying let him die, the beast also ye shall kill."

"She's not a beast—"

Beaudry furiously undid Caelin's belt despite Caelin's savage kicking, flailing, and screaming. He then jammed his hand into Caelin's pants and clenched, fondled, and squeezed Caelin's balls while pressing his raspy face against Caelin's mouth. The oozing stink of Beaudry's breath made Caelin retch. It suddenly all paled to Beaudry's crotch hardening against his ass.

"No!"

"If any man lie with a man se with a woman, both have committed an abomination, let them be put to death."

"NO!"

Beaudry grabbed his dagger and pressed it hard against Caelin's crotch.

"NO!!"

"If thy right hand scandalize thee, cut it off, cast it from thee: for it is better for thee that one of thy members perish, rather than thy whole body be cast into hell."

Caelin struggled more fiercely than ever.

Beaudry lifted and slammed him facefirst into the ground, rendering him semiconscious while again remaining on top of him.

He could hear Beaudry's panting growing heavier and heavier while Beaudry licked his face. And Beaudry seemed to be undoing his own pants.

Beaudry was a shitfuck!

Caelin resumed thrashing and struggling as Beaudry then yanked off Caelin's pack, then pulled up Caelin's armored coat, and despite the ferocity of Caelin's kicking and flailing, tore down Caelin's pants.

"NO!!!"

Caelin twisted and jerked evasively to prevent Beaudry's cock from penetrating his ass.

"NO!!!"

"Do penance therefore for this thy wickedness; and pray to God, that perhaps this thought of thy heart may be forgiven thee..."

Caelin reached as far as he could, in a final act of desperation, until his fingers grasped his pack's shoulder strap. He yanked it closer, grabbed his ice axe, then thrust it backward at Beaudry with all his might. The blunt edge smashed into Beaudry's temple, knocking him out cold.

Caelin scrambled away on all fours while trying to pull up his pants and grab his gear but was too panicked and distraught to do either. He face-planted. Caelin squared away his pants, then his gear. He jumped to his feet, threw on his pack, grabbed Beaudry's guns and ammo clips, and fled faster than he ever had in his life.

What the hell had just happened? Why did stuff like that happen to him? What had he done in a past life to bring on such bad Karma? The world was a vicious and depraved place. Caelin was still not equipped for it, as much as he had started thinking he was. He wanted to just go home. All Dad wanted was to equip him with enough strength and knowledge to get through life without getting fucked in the ass by it, like it had almost happened. Despite all Dad's flaws, despite Dad having been a psycho who had scarred him deeply, Dad had been prophetic in all that he had taught him.

"Weakness invites failure and everything else bad in life," Dad once warned while showing him how to use an ice axe as a weapon. Overhand thrust to the forehead. Side thrust to the throat. Underhanded thrust to the balls. Backward thrust to the temple — like Caelin had just done to Beaudry. At the time, Caelin was sure that Dad had lost his fucking mind due to having lived in Alaska too long.

But weakness indeed had invited failure and everything else bad in his life, Caelin decided about himself.

And he was done inviting it.

Caelin stopped running.

He glared numbly at the ground for a while.

No more weakness.

He went back.

Caelin stood over Beaudry's unconscious body.

Caelin's hands were frighteningly steady. Maybe cause the world was about to be a better place. As much as his soul ached for what he was about to do, there was no going back.

Caelin pointed the gun at Beaudry's chest and fired. Three times. To make sure that shit heart never beat again.

CHAPTER 27

Backtracking that unfamiliar bush was futile. It all looked the same. He'd snuck back the way he'd been dragged, or so he thought. He had no idea where he was. It was suicide. The other two psychos could be lying in ambush for all he knew, alerted by the gunshot blasts that his execution had gone awry since it seemed they executed only by beheading. And then there were those ugly-ass wolf-people running around out there too. Was Daemiana really one of them?

He was feeling ill as the dread of it all lumped drier and drier in his throat. His heart was pounding hardest in his head. The angst knotting his gut made him want to shit. But he kept going instead of retreating. He couldn't let them kill her. He wouldn't. He'd sooner see'em all dead. After all, he was now a killer too. They had *fucked* with the wrong guy.

He was on the right track. Gashing pops and piercing wails echoed in the distance. It had begun! They were killing her! He charged on, full sprint, hellbent on making them pay for everything they ever did to hurt her.

"AAAHHHHHHH!" she cried while hanging from a tree limb by her backwardly shackled, hyper-extended arms.

"Repent!" Ivers demanded while flogging her.

"You repent! For murdering Isabella!" she sobbed.

Ivers whipped Daemiana to the brink of unconsciousness.

Caelin stopped himself from shouting *NO!* as he rushed closer and closer, positioning himself for a sneak attack, stealthily using the trees for cover but unable to stop her agony fast enough. He clutched the gun tighter and tighter as he lurked ever nearer, ever slower, ever quieter. But where the fuck was McConnolly? Was he standing guard somewhere? Was he sneaking up on him from behind or something? Caelin glanced over his shoulder with paranoia as he drew closer and closer.

"Repent so your cursed pact may be broken! Repent!" Ivers demanded of Daemiana.

"It is the Church who must repent, Grand Inquisitor!"

"Repent, Goddamn you!" Ivers grabbed Daemiana's legs and yanked her down steadily. Her shoulder sockets crackled and finally snapped.

"AAAHHHHHHHHHHHHHHHHHHHHHH!"

"Repent now! To save your soul!"

"Only God and His followers," she gasped in excruciation, yet defiant. "Must repent."

"Blasphemy!" Ivers raged and scourged her again to the brink of unconsciousness. "Your cursed pact cannot be fully broken until you repent! If not for your body, then for your eternal soul! Repent!"

Ivers furiously grabbed THE RITUALE ROMANUM from his inner coat pocket and opened it to a section entitled: RITUS EXOR-CIZANDI. He began reciting the Roman Rite of Exorcism in Latin.

"You will fail..." Daemiana said as she teetered in and out of shock. "...as you did with Isabella."

Ivers' voice cracked at the mention of his beloved Isabella. He struggled to continue with the ritual. Daemiana had struck a nerve.

"Jesus Christ, Monsignor! Get ya'self together!" McConnolly chastised while sitting against a nearby tree, clutching his bandaged throat, watching the spectacle in disgust. "She's not fucking possessed! And the other devil bitch was not ya girlfriend!"

"Shut your mouth, Brother McConnolly! I'm not warning you again!"

"End this now! Before ya *fall in love* with and start molesting this devil bitch too!"

Ivers furiously charged McConnolly. They took aim at each other with their guns, looking unhinged.

"Now's your chance, Brother McConnolly."

"Likewise, Monsignor."

Caelin watched with disbelief from behind a nearby tree.

"Return to Rome. Before I kill you," Ivers ordered. "You are re-lieved of duty."

McConnolly staggered to his feet, wobbly, and began to fall, but Ivers held him up by the throat and reassessed the field dressing on the wound.

"You're unfit, Monsignor."

"As are you, Brother McConnolly. As you always have been."

McConnolly just glared back at Ivers.

"Oh yes," Ivers smiled. "I know about the prostitutes you snuck with, en route to and from our missions all around the world, includ-ing Siberia. You Goddamned hypocrite!"

"The world's oldest profession, Monsignor. It pre-dates even ours," McConnolly smirked. "And we can't all be saints like Beaudry."

Saints? Like Beaudry? That ass-fucker, rapist? Either they didn't know, or they were complicit. Neither ignorance nor complicity was acceptable or forgivable!

Ivers' and McConnolly's eyes widened as Caelin furiously jumped out from behind the tree while opening fire. Caelin emptied the entire clip into them as he charged.

Ivers and McConnolly fell and curled into a ball as Caelin reloaded and again unleashed hell on them.

"Saints?!" Caelin screamed. "You're no saints! You're murderers and rapists!"

Caelin again reloaded and emptied another clip into them. He stared at them motionless for a while, struggling to catch his breath. It was over. He reloaded with the final clip, then noticed his second ice axe on the ground nearby, where Beaudry had flanked and beat the shit out of him earlier. Caelin hurriedly retrieved it, affixed it to his pack alongside the other ice axe, and rushed to Daemiana.

He fired at the shackles suspending her from the tree. She fell to the ground. He then shot through her other restraints and helped her up. She was too weak to stand. He lifted her up into his arms and fled.

She gazed up at him weakly, in disbelief, in awe.

He locked eyes with her for a few seconds. Even when covered in blood, and her hair in tangles, with her eyes red and swollen for crying, she was the most beautiful woman he had ever seen.

Caelin forced himself to refocus.

"We gotta keep heading toward the mountains," he whispered soothingly. "Kreuger Sound'll be somewhere on the other side. We're going home."

She closed her eyes.

"You killed them..." Daemiana whispered back.

He said nothing.

A chunk of his soul felt ripped out because of it. Maybe holes in souls healed over time like everything else. But his Karma was irreparably fucked. After murdering those three fuckers, he'd be lucky to come back as a cockroach in the next life. Part of him was okay with it. But another part of him, for the first time, finally understood the allure of atonement and forgiveness; the holy reset button promised by the *faithful*. As much as it was a fucking cop-out, the thought was somewhat soothing.

But Daemiana was his only true north now, in this shitty world where right and wrong had become relative. There was no up or down or left or right anymore. Nothing felt absolute anymore, not even the safe confines of the middle.

How could one do right if there was no wrong? Or how could every attempt at good turn out so bad? After everything he'd done to help Daemiana, it was the act of killing that had finally saved her from them. Why did it have to come that? Why did it have to be that way? Why did people have to treat each other so bad?

To live with himself, Caelin had to accept that it had been the right thing to do, as wrong as it felt in his burning throat, in his churning gut, in his aching lungs, in his numbing heart. It *was* the right thing to do. But *fuck...*

CHAPTER 28

She dashed across the bush like an escaped dove. She then pranced and leaped and twirled. Her fingers caressed the trees she skipped past. Daemiana rejoiced in the increasing swiftness of her healing. The coming full moon was amplifying the curse, including her anomalous powers. But she refused to dwell on the awaiting horrors. She chose to instead celebrate the evaded bears, the dead Inquisitors, and the vanquished Coven. Escape felt within reach, even as Caelin lagged further and further behind, winded and drenched in sweat. She found herself more and more an aficionado of his every step, of his unkilled happenstance, of his tempered wrath. She was alive because of him. It had grown more and more impossible for Daemiana to leave him behind. He was a male like no other — unlikely and inevitable, tragical yet rosy, vilely but sweetly amorous, timid, yet oh so mighty. Caelin was worth waiting. So she did.

He trekked past her without saying a word. His pained stare remained fixed on the looming mountains. He had not so much as looked at her. She was dismayed. Had that been a slight? Was he upset with her? He seemed more different than ever. They had won. Why was he not happy?!

Daemiana trekked alongside him for a while, rummaging for the right words. The silence was infernal and everlong. She tried to understand why he was so far away in mind, heart, and spirit. Males never spoke when it mattered most. It was maddening. She stroked his face to draw him out. He recoiled, she flinched.

"What is wrong?!" she demanded to know.

Were they both too damaged to coincide and coexist, much less flourish together?

"Let's just hurry and get over the m-m-mountains soon."

His stammer made her realize he had not stammered in a long while. Why was he again stammering? Had he suffered a new trauma?

"What happened to you after the Inquisitors separated us?"

"Maybe, just maybe, you ought to stop acting like *n-n-nothing* happened back there. Maybe that'd be the best place to start."

His words struck her like the Inquisitors' scourge. He was upset with her. She slowed to a stop as he trekked on. When males spoke, they often said the wrong thing; hurtful things.

The foot of the mountain range taunted them with scattered ice, jagged rock, and frosty muck. Caelin stumbled and collapsed. He was drenched with sweat and succumbing to exhaustion. She tried to help him up, but he pushed away her hands, wanting only to rest.

"Town's o-o-on the other side somewhere, give or take a few clicks," he panted, appearing far from certain. "We're off course, but we just gotta get over and worry about it later."

She looked up at the mountain ahead of them and sighed. Off course? It appeared so. She had assumed he knew where he was going. The icy mountain was the biggest she had ever seen. It was steeper and more menacing than it had looked from afar. How in Mother's name were they supposed to climb over it? She slowly fixed her disappointed eyes back on Caelin. He rested his head on the muck, beyond disappointed in himself as well. He did not need the weight of her disappointment on him too.

"Weakness invites everything bad in life..." he mumbled quietly to himself.

"We can rest."

"I-I-I'm fine."

"We should rest—"

"I'm not weak!" he exploded and punched the ground, gashing his fist.

She was taken aback by his sudden burst of rage. It seemed to have come out of nowhere.

"I am not saying you are—"

"Everyone thinks I'm weak!"

"I do not believe that—"

"Yeah? Y-Y-You knew those things were coming." Caelin finally stood, referring to the Coven. "But you didn't say shit! Cause you think I'm weak. Well, guess what, n-n-not only can I stomach the truth, I'm still here! Alive!"

She was at a loss for words.

"Who were those fucking wolf-people?!" he demanded. "Who was the main one, the one who tried to kill you?!"

"I do not like you're tone."

"Who is he?!"

"I told you to flee and go far, far away! Did I not?!"

"Cause you think I'm weak!"

"Because the Coven devours the strongest of the strong!"

"I can handle myself and the truth, whatever it is!"

She turned her back to him, defiant. The truth never helped any-thing.

Caelin walked around and faced her.

"Why do your people want y-you dead?"

"They are not my people!"

He glared at her, demanding the truth.

"Not anymore..." she conceded, looking away again and sighing. "Dionisio was a former love. Long before our accurst existence."

"So, that big, scary fuck was your boyfriend?" Caelin blurted out jealously.

"He is not my anything!" she replied, fearing she had to concede more truth or risk losing Caelin's trust. "Not anymore."

"Not *anymore*?"

"I betrayed Dionisio and the rest of our Coven when I left them to seek a cure by breaking the Coven's cursed pact. They will never understand or accept that. It was the ultimate betrayal. That is why they desire to kill me."

Caelin glared pensively out into the distance.

"Why don't they wanna be cured too?"

She hesitated. Therein lied the worst truth of all.

"Continued immortality. Continued dominion over Mother Nature."

The words appeared to knock the wind out of him. It had proven too much truth, too soon. She braced herself. Would he ask if he had heard right? Immortality? How could she ever explain her being born thousands of moon cycles ago, in medieval Italy, during the Church's Papal Inquisition? How would he react? Instead...

"Who was Isabella?"

That was not the question she expected. It was complicated.

"Nothing good will come of this talk—"

"Was she in your coven?" he asked.

"Yes," she sighed.

"Was she your mother?"

There was tense silence.

"Your sister?"

The silence grew tenser.

"Your friend?"

The silence grew tensest and finally ruptured.

"Isabella, too, was a former love, like Dionisio. Long before our accurst existence."

"Wh-Wh-What?"

"That was another reason why the Church hated our nature-worship Coven. We were fluid in all ways. We rejected all conventions. We embraced all love, all ritual enlightenment and spirituality. Before it took a dark turn."

He seemed unable to absorb any more truth.

He simply stared up blankly at the looming peak, then drew his ice axes and crampons from his pack.

"Whatever the fuck all that means..." he replied.

"I am now yours," she assured him. "All yours."

Caelin simply embarked up the mountain.

Had she lost all allure? Had she killed some notion of her in his mind? Was he really only then learning that love came in all forms and did not conform to a single ideal? Who was he to judge her?! That was the Inquisitors' way of thinking! Males knew nothing of love! Love, like God, was a failed ideal. Things were simply as they were! All one could ever hope for in life was a fleeting reprieve from the misery that was existence. But to that silly boy, love appeared to be so much more. Or so he would have her believe. Was she really to think that love could mean everything to a male, perhaps even something long-lasting and grounded in kindness of heart and generosity of spirit? Did he believe her stupid?! She knew better. That was what the followers of God proclaimed love to be! Yet always, so tragically and hypocritically, their so-called *love* fell so short in their actions! Caelin was a fool and a hopeless aficionado for all things silly if he believed love to be anything more than a momentary alignment of interests.

And yet, for some reason, as ridiculous as he was, she found herself rushing up the mountain after him.

CHAPTER 29

He stumbled over and around jagged rocks and eventually crossed the snow line. The terrain had become increasingly vertical. Up ahead, by mid-mountain, it was. His apprehension was elsewhere, though, as his mind whirled over everything that had happened, over everything that had been said. Not the right mindset before a treacherous climb. But he was as livid as he was spent. A jealous rage was fueling him, and his pride refused to let him stop for a rest. All because she'd become tarnished in his mind, polluted somehow. She was no longer his and never was. She belonged to her Coven, to Isabella, to Dionisio. To every fucking one except him. Was it even fair to feel that way? Caelin wanted to explode. Was this love? Cause it sucked. Cause it was toxic. Cause it was a lethal pipedream. Cause the cost was too high. He should have been planning his siege upon the summit. Instead, he understood why Hermit Lawson was happier alone. And why some long-dead philosophers had rightfully concluded that: *hell was other people* or that *the road to hell was paved by good intentions.*

Caelin's legs buckled from exhaustion, and he fell to his knees. He was wheezing and gasping for air. Lack of acclimatization was the biggest bitch. He wasn't thinking straight. He needed to calm down and focus. He stared up at the summit. It was easily 19,000 or 20,000 feet in elevation. Maybe, 18 and change, if he was lucky. It'd be his first high altitude, vertical ascent without Dad to save his ass if it went south. Which meant he would probably die unless he turned around and found the friendly ridge he used to traverse the mountains the first time.

Caelin sat down, wiped his brow, and caught his breath.

Daemiana sat beside him. Her brow was dry. Her breath was calm. Her wounds had healed. No scar, no gash, not a scratch on her. She rested her head on his shoulder.

Caelin found himself unable to stay peeved at her.

She ran her fingers over the crampon spikes affixed to his boots.

"Sure you're good to climb like that?" he asked her, staring at her bare feet, unable to get used to it.

She shrugged nonchalantly—

Daemiana jumped up and gasped in horror.

"The Coven!"

"Where's the rest?!" Caelin jumped up as he looked around.

LeVee and Mikaela were charging up the mountain with superhuman speed. The others were nowhere to be seen.

Caelin frantically thrust his ice axes and crampon spikes into the ice as he climbed the ever-increasingly vertical face. No belay meant certain death if he fell.

Daemiana clawed her way up alongside him with ease and animal-like agility.

"Save yourself! Cut out of here!" Caelin panted. "Get back to town and tell the Bishop everything!"

"I am not leaving you!"

"No sense in you dying too!"

"We shall die together, then!"

LeVee and Mikaela were rapidly gaining.

High altitude gusts pounded the vertical, mid-mountain face. The windchill ripped him to his core while the force nearly plucked him off the mountain to his death.

Daemiana lost her grip. Caelin grabbed her wrist before she fell.

"Loose ice," Caelin warned and glanced down. "Careful."

Just then, a devious gleam came over his eyes as LeVee and Mikaela rapidly closed in on them.

"*Loose* ice..." he said again as he frantically thrust a climbing cam into an exposed rock crevice. "Go on without me!"

"I am not leaving you!" she said.

"Do it! Now!" Caelin demanded while securing his belay to the cam.

Daemiana reluctantly climbed on as Caelin kicked and pounded the mountain face with all his might, over and over and over, with growing desperation. The huge ice sheet he was on dislodged and fell, with him on it.

Caelin's fall was arrested by the line as the ice smashed down on LeVee and Mikaela, knocking them off the mountain. Caelin dangled on the line and watched with elated disbelief as they plunged hundreds of feet. Holy shit. It worked!

LeVee thrust his claws into the ice and eventually arrested his fall while Mikaela continued falling and cartwheeling thousands of feet until she smashed headfirst into the toe of the mountain. Her steaming blood spattered, and her skull, spine, and innards pulverized against the rocks. She let out a hideous shriek that boomed all the way back up the mountain. But her accelerated, supernatural healing slowed and eventually stopped all bleeding as her bones crackled back into place. Her compound fractures sunk and snapped back together beneath her torn, mangled flesh and skin. Every part of her fused and healed fast. She scurried back up the mountain not long after.

Caelin and Daemiana closed in on the summit, with LeVee still in hot pursuit.

An ominous rumble halted their ascent.

"Avalanche..." Caelin said in horror. "Any moment now..."

"Mother, no, please. Show us mercy," Daemiana begged of the mountain.

"Only the summit can save us now," Caelin decided and resumed his frantic ascent. "Let's go!"

"Mother Nature's wrath is again imminent!" Daemiana cried. "She hates me and my kind!"

"Faster!

They eventually crawled onto the summit with LeVee mere seconds away. Caelin then screamed at the top of his lungs and pounded the ice frantically with his ice axes, deliberately causing the rumble to grow louder and louder until it gave way to a huge, deafening avalanche. It devoured LeVee and blew Caelin and Daemiana down the opposite side of the mountain.

Caelin thrust one axe into the ice and held on to Daemiana with his other arm, managing to barely arrest their violent tumble. He exhaled a long, billowy sigh of incredulous relief, only inches from a ledge and the underlying void. They should have been dead. But yet, somehow, they weren't.

Caelin looked down. The coast awaited them 20,000 feet below, in the distance. It never looked more breathtaking. Yet, Daemiana was only staring at him in awe.

"You are not weak," she breathed warmly into his ear.

"What?" he gasped, his heart still in his throat.

"You are the strongest male I have ever known."

But Caelin knew he had just been futilely lucky, not badass. It was only a matter of time before his luck would finally run out. Death was undoubtedly imminent.

He let out an exhausted, agonized sigh.

"I believe in you, wholly," Daemiana said and held onto him tightly.

She again gave him the strength to go on.

CHAPTER 30

An arduous descent amid whipping gusts and icy flurries fed them into the ambrosial belly of a coastal woodland, where piney aromas interlaced with briny mists from the not-so-distant ocean. She closed her eyes and inhaled deeply to let it all in. The chill had become less mauling. Ode to Mother's gentler side. Daemiana reopened her eyes slowly and eased back into the moment and task at hand.

Not a clue hailed which way town lie or the extent of the remaining journey. So, she waited. Caelin was inching along, step by stubby step, stymied by his own mortality, unable to keep up. He collapsed onto a meandering brook and slurped insatiably, pausing only to gasp for air. He dipped his sunburnt, weather-beaten face into the water, rolled onto his back, and stared up at the sky while trying to catch his breath. Never had she seen anyone so deathly tired. Was her cursed fix so accurst if it spared her such pain? Yes, she had long decided. Contrary to the vehement sentiments of her wicked Coven.

An array of wildflowers caught her attention while Caelin rested. She was lured like a curious child on a spring day. Daemiana lay among them and watched them wiggle in the breeze. Bliss. It was not long before they shriveled and withered away, reminding her that she was still an abomination, unworthy of them.

Flowers were what she missed most. And songbirds too, which never chirped when she was around. Mother, at Her most beautiful, had shunned Daemiana. Only Mother's beasts sought her now to destroy her, often going against their very natures. It was nature behaving unnaturally to destroy the unnatural. Oh, why was Mother so uncompromising and unforgiving? It was that dire longing for a return to grace in Mother's eyes which compelled Daemiana most to leave the Coven.

She pounced up onto her tiptoes and swayed and twirled and pranced and danced as wonderfully as she could for Mother. It was all Daemiana could offer Her. Perhaps, she could one day cajole Mother's forgiveness—

"You're so alive," Caelin doted, savoring her every swanlike motion.

Daemiana had forgotten she was not alone. She wrapped her cloak around herself tight to deny his prying eyes.

"As are you," she replied and skipped and leapt and whirled.

Caelin grabbed a wildflower and pressed it against his nose as if trying to better understand her joy. He inhaled deeply, never once taking his eyes off her.

"No. You're free. That's what I meant."

"As are you," she replied while gyring like a crimson-shrouded ballerina.

Caelin tossed the wildflower into the brook and watched it meander away.

"No," he moaned as if coming to that realization. "It's like...I'm afraid all the time. Of everything. And angry at everyone. Can't even remember when I wasn't. I'm not alive or free."

Daemiana just continued dancing, unsure what he meant by those vexing words. Caelin was being silly. He was breathing, was he not? In this beautiful place! And he was the mightiest knight she had ever known! He had helped her escape the beasts. He vanquished the slayers. He defeated LeVee and Mikaela on the mountain!

"It's like, all my life, I let everything hold me back," he sighed.

But how? He had proven himself unstoppable, she thought.

"From what?" she asked.

Caelin approached pensively. He tried to embrace her. She pulled away and continued to dance, but he held on. He took her into his arms.

"From getting what I want, that's what," he said. "Not until right fucking now. I'm here, doing exactly what I want, on my own terms; that's what I'm trying to say."

She smiled, still unsure what he was getting at.

"There's nowhere else I wanna be, except here with you."

Her smile slowly dissipated. Oh no...

She looked away.

Had he finally called her bluff? Was he making a declaration of love? How was that possible? Males were incapable of *real* love. She wanted love, real love, but it was terrifying. Males only took, never reciprocated in those ways. That was how she justified not truly loving them, or being wholly honest with them, or ever staying very long with them. They deserved that. Betrayal was all they knew, and she could not give them what they wanted most. Caelin was turning everything upside down! She was again losing control—

"For the first time in my life, I know what I really want! That's what I'm saying," Caelin rejoiced and kissed her.

Was he out of his mind? He did not know her. Not truly. She found herself unable to look anywhere else but down.

"The cursed pact..." she sighed.

"We're gonna break it."

"The Inquisitors—"

"They're dead."

"The spiritual treatment—"

"The Bishop'll know what to do once we get back to town."

Daemiana had not anticipated it all moving so fast. She wasn't ready. She wanted more than anything to believe him. But Caelin had yet to ask — truly ask — why she was the way she was or what she and her coven had done to bring upon themselves the wicked curse. He was far from knowing everything. Perhaps, deep in his heart, he did not want to know.

"What if the cursed pact cannot be broken?" she sighed, needing to know if Caelin really knew what he was saying and if he truly meant it. "What if it is incurable?"

His silence was telling.

"I cannot give you what you want."

"What does that even mean?" he replied unbeknownst.

Caelin was failing to consider the totality of the situation. He was assuming a happy ending. She fought desperately to stop herself from saying any more. Males were best kept in the dark about such things. But then again, if he truly loved her, would he not understand? She found herself unsure why she so badly wanted his love to be real and able to survive the truth, any truth, even as her better judgment warned against such fallacies.

"We sought immortality and great, great power through an ancient pagan ritual; a pact," she confessed before she could stop herself. "The dark turn it took; the price was ritual human sacrifice and the eating of human flesh and the drinking of human blood. Not unlike what the Church does during communion."

He looked as perplexed as he did, disgusted.

"A Black Mass...?"

"The ritual finally succeeded. The Great Spirit granted us great power and immortality. By making us what we are."

"Maneaters?" he replied while staring at her in horror.

She nodded reluctantly. "The pact was a curse. It was a betrayal. That is why I cannot be yours. Because I am His. Body and soul."

The color left Caelin's face, "Wh-Wh-Who's He?"

"I cannot be yours, fully and completely yours, until the cursed pact with Him is broken."

"Him who? What *Great Spirit*?"

Caelin shook his head as he stepped back, struggling to wrap his mind around it, mumbling mostly to himself, "There are no *spirits*. All there is Karma; energies. We can work our way out of this mess..."

"It was selfish and abominable of us to seek dominion over nature, as we did. I know that now. It is why Mother Nature turned against us."

Caelin backed away, looking physically ill, his eyes reddening, not wanting to hear anymore.

"That is why I no longer serve the Great Spirit. The curse is NOT something I wanted!"

"Who the fuck is this Great Spirit?!"

He did not want to know. Yet, he knew. Deep inside, he had to know. That the Great Spirit was who the Inquisitors called: *Satan.*

"I will be yours fully — in heart, mind, and body — when the cursed pact is broken," Daemiana assured him as she approached and caressed his face.

"If, like you said, it can be broken," he sighed and resumed the journey without looking at her. "And if you *really* want it to be broken."

"I want it to be broken! How dare you doubt that?!"

The truth had again pulled them apart. It was ruining everything, as always! Never again!

Caelin stormed back.

"From the start, the lines got blurred, cause you blurred'em. When all I wanted was to help, you got into m-m my fucking head, and let me think I had a real shot with you! That's what happened! That's what's really going on here. So, let's cut the bullshit."

He stormed off.

"I told you to flee and forget me! I told you I could not give you what you wanted!"

"The Bishop'll fix your problems once we get back to town!" Caelin yelled back. "That's all there's left to do! So you can start fucking with his head! You won't need me anymore!"

How dare he say that to her?

"Asshole!" she screamed in response to his vulgarity, knowing only that the word was used in anger by vulgars like him.

Daemiana paced around, clutching her face, refusing to shed a single tear. She screamed. She hated him! Why, oh why, had she told him the truth?! Her pride was succumbing to her cold little heart. She knew he would have helped her whether or not she had played the coquette. But it was better, and it still was better, to have him wrapped around her finger. Caelin had proclaimed his love for her after more than proving it over and over. Could he, and his love for her, survive another night? She hoped so in that moment and rushed after him. He was her knight in shining armor. And as flawed and as damaged as they each were, together they could and would make things right. She was sure of it.

CHAPTER 31

THE SOUND'S FISHY BREEZE NUZZLED AND SOOTHED HER. JOURNEY'S end was near, and evening not far behind. A sparse fog was creeping in from the eerily still Pacific. The outskirts of town greeted them with uneasy solace. Her heart slowly sank. Not a single noise was within earshot, and not a soul was in sight. The safe-haven Caelin had promised felt somehow fouled. Something was wrong. But she said nothing. At the moment, she was more concerned about lingering silence and tension between them.

Their pride was proving insurmountable, though. He had not spoken to her; she had not spoken to him in a long while. The remnants of their fragile alliance could not survive any more strain, so she held her tongue and glanced out at the ocean, then up at the sky. There were no birds. Not so much as a wayward gull. She looked down. Waves of disordered ants were fleeing town; no chaos, no single file, only every ant for itself in mass exodus. There was no doubt anymore. She had to say something.

Daemiana swallowed her pride and turned to Caelin, who was still intent on not looking at her.

"Stop," she whispered. "We must go back."

"We're almost home—"

Spattered blood and claw marks gradually came into view, on the ground, on homes, everywhere.

The dread in Caelin's eyes anguished her most as he slowly realized what she already knew. Would he blame her?

Scattered body parts came into view. Men, women, children. All torn apart. Carnage in all directions. Bloody innards hung from a pole like lurid ornaments. Brave flies buzzed about, feasting. Kreuger Sound had been slaughtered. Caelin looked too emotionally eviscerated to understand, much less believe, what he was seeing.

"The Coven did this," she whispered if he didn't already know. "While LeVee and Mikaela pursued us up the mountain, Dionisio and Cybilia were likely en route here. To do this..."

The buzzing stopped. The flies were gone.

A roar and a woman's scream slashed the silence.

Caelin and Daemiana flinched. They fled to the kennel-barn abutting the Sheriff's Post. Caelin yanked open the heavy double-doors as the roar and screams drew near. They rushed inside and shut the double-doors behind them. The search-and-rescue hounds barked, the horses neighed. All were agitated in their pens.

Caelin and Daemiana peered out through a crack in the wooden barn wall.

A young woman was fleeing for her life.

Dionisio and Cybilia were gaining with superhuman speed. They knocked her down, toying with her, relishing her torment.

"Help me, someone! Please!" she screamed.

"It's Lori!" Caelin whispered. "I gotta help!"

"No! They will kill us!"

Dionisio's and Cybilia's cackles boomed diabolically as they stood over Lori.

"She's my friend!" Caelin drew his gun and silver dagger and rushed the doors. "I gotta help!"

Daemiana grabbed him.

"You cannot help her!"

"You still think I'm weak? After everything?!"

"Weakness has nothing to do with this!"

"I can save her!"

"You cannot! You are not fast enough! You are not strong enough! The Coven is mightier than the beasts, mightier than the Inquisitors!"

Caelin's mortality bore reminding, as mighty as he was.

"They killed my fucking town! I'm not gonna let'em kill her too!" he raged.

Daemiana accepted that there'd be no convincing him otherwise, so she rushed the rear door before Caelin could stop her, refusing to let him kill himself.

"I will lead them away, then!"

"What?!"

"Take the girl to the chapel and hide! The Coven will not enter the chapel!"

"Wait!"

Daemiana dashed away with superhuman speed.

Dionisio clawed Lori.

Cybilia grabbed her hair and thrust her into the air.

Lori hit the ground headfirst, unconscious.

Their sadistic cackles again broke the thick silence.

They then pounced on Lori and opened their jaws to devour her—

"Leave her be!"

Dionisio and Cybilia slowly turned.

Daemiana was there, before them, nauseated by the stale rank of the townspeoples' blood all over them. Her stomach was turned most by the memory of being like them not long ago, before the Grand Inquisitor's spiritual treatment.

Daemiana backed away as they approached.

"Leave her be, Mia?" Dionisio snarled.

"These poor people did not deserve this. They were not Inquisitors."

"You never understood and respected thy alpha, Miana. That is what led you astray."

"You are no alpha. You are a slave. We all are, to the cursed pact."

His laughter boomed and echoed well into the distance.

"You are an aficionado of evil, an extremist, no better than the Inquisitors," Daemiana chided.

"You always were willful and full of capriccio, Mia. And you went as far as to betray our sacred gift."

"Gift? This vile curse over us? A curse is all the pact will ever be!"

"A pact you sought to break, Miana, when you allowed the Inquisitors to capture you alive; something which is gravely forbidden. Now, the Great Spirit awaits your soul."

"He betrayed us first! When He made us into these things!"

"You behoove me, Mia. Woe is you."

"My name is Daemiana, and my spirit is my own!"

"Great power and immortality. Dominion over nature. How unbearable, Mia," Dionisio mocked.

"I will be a cursed abomination no longer. I desire to again love and be loved!"

"Love?!" Dionisio growled. "Is something a putain like you never understood."

"The pact was a terrible mistake—"

"You were, are, and always will be, a fickle whore! Unable to commit to anything!"

His loathsome slurs seared her like an Inquisitor's silver blade. No insult was more oppressive than *whore*. Males hated females in paradoxes; for loving them, for not loving them, for giving in to them, for not. Vulgarity of that kind was best met with vulgarity.

"You are Satan's lapdog! A vile Devil bitch!" she replied lividly, as the Inquisitor McConnolly had once said to her. "That is all you will ever be!"

Dionisio was laughing no longer.

"He awaits your soul after I tear off your head!" Dionisio charged.

Daemiana sprinted away, toward the docks, with Dionisio and Cybilia in hot pursuit, all moving at superhuman speed. Daemiana glanced over her shoulder, past Dionisio and Cybilia. Caelin stormed out of hiding, yanked Lori up into his arms, and rushed off toward the chapel.

It was done. Her martyrdom would soon be complete. There would be no surviving Dionisio and Cybilia. The Coven, like the Inquisitors, were driven by fervency alone. The only fruit their kind bore was condemnation and destruction of those who were different. Opposing it had proven futile. Daemiana labored to make her peace with it all as their bestial grunts drew closer and closer and closer. It would soon be over.

CHAPTER 32

They ripped their claws into her back and tore her down to the ground. The swiveling fury of her kicking, scratching and biting enabled her to break free long enough to scramble away before they could kill her. She resumed her frantic sprint with Dionisio and Cybilia again rapidly gaining. Daemiana refused to die without taking one or both with her.

She blew past the docks and noticed—

Huge, black dorsal fins circling a nearby iceberg, stalking the seals basking on it. Mother's deadliest beasts of all: killer whales. Daemiana dove into the frigid sea and swam toward them with all her might. Dionisio and Cybilia dove in after her with an unwavering intent for her blood.

With certain death all around, Daemiana swam for dear life and eventually reached the iceberg. The orcas had dispersed due to the sudden, abominable presence. Daemiana clawed her way up onto the ice as the orcas regrouped and charged hyper-aggressively. The seals flopped away from Daemiana and dove into the sea in panicked droves, more terrified of her than of their natural predators.

An anomalous killing frenzy ensued. The orcas' massive dorsal fins wobbled high above the water as their jaws mangled apart hopeless flesh, churning the sea a frothy red.

Daemiana held on to the ice as it swayed violently. She looked for Dionisio and Cybilia in the bloody carnage, wondering if the killer whales were devouring them along with the seals like she'd hoped would happen—

They pounced on her from behind, tore her down to the ice, and pinned her facedown.

"No!" Daemiana cried.

She thrust her claws into the ice and dragged herself and them closer to the edge of the ice.

"Mother, please! Mother! HELP ME, MOTHER!" Daemiana screamed at the orcas.

Dionisio grabbed her head with his powerful claws while Cybilia held down her arms. Before Dionisio could tear off her head, an orca pounced onto the ice and tore into Cybilia's legs. It thrashed her about hideously, like a grizzly laying siege to a salmon. Cybilia let out a booming shriek as Dionisio released Daemiana, leapt forward, and grabbed Cybilia's arms. He held on to Cybilia with all his superhuman might to stop the massive blackfish from dragging her back into the sea. Dionisio suddenly fell back, holding Cybilia's upper body. The orca receded back into the red froth with Cybilia's legs in its jaws. Dearest mother...

Daemiana leapt to her feet as the orca's brethren bumped the ice, intent on knocking them all into the sea and into their jaws. She stumbled around, off-balance, and tumbled toward the opposite edge of the iceberg before arresting her slide with her claws.

Other orcas pounced onto the ice, each more intent on blood than the last. Dionisio clawed them back with demonic fury.

Mother's wrath proved fiercer than Daemiana could have ever imagined. Daemiana had grossly underestimated the extent of the peril she had provoked with the killer whales. With no choice left, with her seconds on the ice numbered, she gave herself a long-running start and leaped high into the air, over the adjacent orcas, and crashed into the sea.

She swam frantically back toward the mainland.

Two orcas were in rapid pursuit and gaining fast.

The first chomped her thighs and dragged her into the depths while thrashing her viciously. Daemiana clawed relentlessly at its eye until landing a direct hit, rupturing it. The orca let go.

Daemiana resurfaced, gasping for air. Just then—

She saw the seven-foot dorsal fin of the other orca swooshing toward her like a giant blade. She jerked aside with a sudden burst of speed, dodging its jaws. The killer whale blew by. She managed to thrust her claws into its flank. The orca's momentum towed her at immense speed toward shore. The water beast's power was like nothing she had ever felt.

Daemiana let go as the orca dove down into the depths. She resumed swimming as fast as she could, and eventually scrambled onto the cobbly sands of the shore, barely evading other orcas' jaws as they beached themselves violently in one final attempt to kill her.

Daemiana crawled away, bleeding profusely from the legs. She collapsed behind a boulder, exhausted and sobbing. Mother's water beasts had saved her by nearly killing her. The goodness of Mother's equilibrium knew no bounds. Mother was the only absolute truth. And there were no greater works than Hers.

<h1 style="text-align:center">CHAPTER 33</h1>

THE CHAPEL WAS UNSCATHED. ITS CROSS REIGNED OVER THE CARNAGE like some darkling beacon. Caelin glared at it, standing just shy of the bethel steps with Lori in his arms. How could this have happened? Nothing was left. It was good Dad was dead, no longer around to see his beloved Kreuger Sound this way; all his lifelong friends and their families so horribly killed. Tragedy and heartbreak were the only constants in life. Caelin needed the cosmic rationales for all that had happened more than ever. Why was the world was such shit? Were there any absolute truths in life? Or was it all a hopeless abyss of misery and despair?

Caelin kicked open the chapel doors.

He stepped into the darkness and set Lori down on the rear pew. He remained in the center aisle, glaring at the alter. The flickery red of the sanctuary lamp jounced and thrashed and beat back the smothering black. Caelin's aversion to the place was gone. He was ready to confront whatever was there. He approached slowly. Whether some cold, impersonal karmic justice awaited him or whether some fiery, almighty judgment loomed, he was ready.

"Why?" Caelin asked, demanding to know. "Why?!"

Instead, the cosmic silence was as deafening as ever. Its void was deeper than deep, and its pitch black was lonely and cold when not outright terrifying. As always, the misery of the silence was kaleidoscopic, and its nothingness monolithic. *That* was why Caelin did not pray or meditate. The chasm's unbearable quiet was as agonizing as the misery that was life. There was no refuge from the pain, anywhere. Everyone had long been forsaken. All lines were blurred beyond recognition. Good and evil were irreconcilable distinctions without differences, wholly dependent on the day and the side one was on. Was it all truly and absolutely relative then? Were there truly such things as good works? And did the chaos and confusion arise from nothingness or from an unjust higher power who bestowed scraps willy-nilly?

Caelin was futilely lost and adrift in the vast cosmic sea. Mere doubt or contentment would have been a welcomed relief if only he were wired that way. He couldn't commit to anything short of certainty, but nothing was certain. The cowardly paralysis that had plagued Caelin in daily life plagued him spiritually as well—

He realized the floor was goopy to the step.

Caelin flicked on his headlamp and looked down.

It was blood.

He drew his gun and dagger and looked around.

A dark figure was seated on the front pew, off to the side.

Caelin backed away, readying to flee, stopped himself, and instead pressed forward.

Raspy mumblings in Latin became discernible.

"Bishop...?" Caelin realized who it was and rushed to him.

The Bishop's eyes were gouged out. Much of his face and scalp hung from his head in shreds. Somehow, he was still alive.

"It's me, Caelin. The groundskeeper—"

"I couldn't help... When the screams began, I went outside... I couldn't help," the Bishop rambled on and on, drifting into shock.

Caelin gently grasped his mauled hands.

"I know what did this, Bishop."

"A carnal, demonic manifestation... I must call Rome."

"Rome?"

"To inform them..."

"Of what?"

"The Secret Order of Slayers have failed..."

"Who?"

"Present-era...Crusaders, Templars, Inquisitors—"

"Inquisitors?" Caelin stammered as his heart sank.

"Now everyone is dead," the Bishop rambled on, too badly in shock to maintain any high secrecy.

"Th-Th-Those three psychos? What are you saying, Bishop?"

"The Church must send more."

Caelin grew nauseous.

"Those killers were sent here?! To help?!"

The Slayers' repeated warnings rang loud in Caelin's head over and over, demanding that he stop interfering and instead help evacuate the town.

"Is this all my fault, Bishop? Cause I stopped them from killing her? Is that what you're saying?!"

"Take me to a phone at once, my son—"

"Is that what you're saying, Bishop?!" Caelin pleaded.

"A phone! Now, my son."

Caelin stumbled back, hyperventilating.

"I had to help her. I couldn't let them kill her. I was doing what was right!"

"Outside of God's Grace...nothing is right."

"What does that even mean?!" Caelin raged, remembering enough Sunday School to know he'd always struggled with that premise. *God* did not own all that was good and right!

The Bishop coughed and gagged uncontrollably, vomiting blood.

"Bishop—"

"Good Works are not always feasible," the Bishop gasped. "Sometimes Faith Alone is all there is left. That is the Slayers' unofficial creed, as heretical and unbiblical as it is…"

"So what is right and what is wrong then, Bishop?!"

Caelin paced around, clutching his head in despair.

He fell to his knees.

"She just wanted to be free of the curse!" Caelin raged. "By breaking the pact!"

The Bishop had keeled off to the side. Caelin lurched forward, grabbed him, and lowered him to the floor.

"Bishop! I need answers!"

Caelin pressed his fingers against the Bishop's neck. Nothing, no pulse. Caelin compressed the Bishop's chest over and over and over.

"How do I to make things right?!"

The compressions became furious, incessant pounding.

"Bishop!" Caelin screamed at the cosmic silence. "Please!"

The Bishop was dead, and there was no bringing him back. Had it all been all for absolutely nothing, everything Caelin had done? All because he'd been wrong? Always wrong! Wrong about every fucking thing!

"I was just doing the right thing!"

CHAPTER 34

CAELIN WALLOWED OUT OF THE CHAPEL ONTO THE BLOODY MUCK. He no longer bothered stepping over the scattered flesh as he lumbered into the heart of town, his gait meandering unsteadily, his eyes glassy and aimless. The aching hot in his throat made it hard to breathe and impossible to swallow. The coppery smell of blood lingered nauseatingly. Buzzing flies circled him like tiny vultures.

Was this how fanatics *found* God? Rock bottom, in the stinking red slop and shit of their own making? Maybe, the hypocrites' *Faith Alone* was the ultimate submission to that, a declaration of total helplessness and depravity, a complete deferring of all control to *Him*. Then, as long as one had *true* Faith, whatever one did, no matter how shitty, it was all just God's *will*; God acting through us. No free will, just God's will.

Caelin fell to his knees and puked. He retched and coughed violently for a while. He needed all that invisible weight off of him. Before it killed him. He was done with it. All of it. Even Karma, which had made the most sense to him. He was letting go of all of it. Higher

Power or not, Caelin's life was in his own hands. That had never been clearer. It was his own judgment, his own conscience, and what he wanted that mattered now. It was his life. And his death, when it came, would be on his own terms. Any cosmic reality outside of that would have to catch up and do its part. Or not.

A hideous chill rolled in along with the sparse fog as day was succumbing to twilight.

Caelin waited in the jail, in an open cell. His sights were fixed on Deputy Bob's eviscerated corpse on the floor outside the cell. A rifle was clasped by what was left of Deputy Bob's hand. His other arm was gone. His nose and mouth were mauled off too. What was left of his broken, coffee-stained teeth were no longer yellow and instead resembled red porcelain. His eyes were locked in a state of pure terror. Not long ago, the sight of that would have scarred Caelin for life.

Then, out of nowhere, she was back, soaking wet, standing over the corpse.

"Why are you not in the chapel?" Daemiana asked. "I was calling out for you."

He couldn't get himself to look at her. He was in the throes of hating himself and resenting her for the massacre. And if he was going to end up like Deputy Bob, it sure as shit wouldn't be in the swivel of Daemiana's jaws and claws. He was going to make sure of it.

"Go to the chapel at once!" she demanded. "You will be safe there!"

But he continued glaring at her feet, avoiding her eyes. She was standing on a portion of Deputy Bob's scattered entrails as if nothing, gobs of bloody shit oozing out. Only a psycho could be at ease with that. He wondered if he really knew her or if he ever could.

"Where is the girl?"

What? Lori... He'd forgotten about her. After setting her down in the chapel, he had failed to check on her condition. Was she okay? Was she still alive? That shameful failure was too embarrassing to admit. And it only infuriated him more. So he refused to answer. He would not be pushed around by Daemiana. No matter how much he loved her.

The silence crescendoed.

He decided to go through with it.

Daemiana angrily rushed into the cell and grabbed him.

"Where is she?! I almost died saving you both!"

Caelin furiously stormed past her and slammed the cell door shut behind him. He'd succeeded in locking her up as planned. He needed Daemiana out of the way for the night, so he could do what he needed to do without fear of being killed by her.

"Why are you doing this, Caelin? Are you betraying me too?" she cried, assuming the worse. "What happened to your people is not my fault! I never meant for this to happen," she pleaded and reached for him through the bars.

"The road to hell is paved by good intentions," Caelin rasped. "I now understand what it means."

"Please..."

He struggled to find the right words. He wasn't blaming her, and he wasn't giving up on her.

"The Coven will kill us both!" she cried. "I'm trapped here!"

"I'm gonna kill'em all," Caelin vowed. "It's all I want now. I'm gonna fucking kill'em all!"

"Do not be a fool! Let me out and then save yourself by hiding in the chapel for the night. You will be safe there. In the morning, if we are still alive, we can take one of the boats and go far, far away—"

"No more running. It all ends tonight."

"You cannot win!"

After everything they'd been through, after everything she'd said, that was how she truly felt. He just nodded with a solemn acceptance. She pleaded to be let out while Caelin pried the rifle from Deputy Bob's cold, dead hand. He then left the jail without so much as looking back, bent only on vengeance.

The remnant red horizon dwindled and succumbed to the full moon and aurora borealis. Caelin was out in the open, in the center of town, waiting for the inevitable. He was contemplating attack, escape, and counterattack positions, all relative to the refuge of the chapel. Not that he knew anything about the soundness of his plan. What he did know was the town, like the back of his hand.

His armored coat was snugly buttoned up to his throat, and the coat's hood was tightly draped over his head, the way the Inquisitors had worn theirs in battle. He was clutching his silver dagger in one hand and his ice axe in the other. His pack and rifle were strapped to his back, and his gun was in his coat pocket. Whether the fight took them in and around the chapel or up onto the rooftops or up into the mountains, he was ready.

Something became discernible through the fog. He gripped his weapons tighter. His heart began pounding. But his legs grew weak at the sight of the impossible. The Inquisitors were approaching, guns drawn, eyeing the carnage with fury, looking intent on wrath. That was not possible. His exhausted mind was hallucinating. Caelin closed his eyes tight, demanding that his mind get its shit together.

Caelin opened his eyes to see that the slayers had spotted him and were charging. The fiery flashes of their gunfire lit up the infant night, knocking him over. He'd been hit! They were real! How?! He tried to sit up, but they were already upon him, reloading. They again opened fired and emptied their clips into him. He gasped and wheezed for air, feeling it all going black. They had finally gotten him.

McConnolly yanked Caelin's head up by the hair, "The coats are bulletproof, stupid! In case ya wonder'in why everyone, including yourself, is still breathe'in!" he raged. "Which is more than I can say for your townspeople, ya stupid fuck! Ya hands are soaked with their blood!"

Beaudry pressed his gun against Caelin's forehead, "Fear not those things which thou shalt suffer. Be FAITHful till DEATH: I will give thee the crown of life."

Ivers lowered Beaudry's gun, "No. Only by dying at the Coven's jaws tonight will he truly understand the gravity of what he's done. I'd otherwise put the bullet in his head myself."

Caelin was on the brink of unconsciousness, struggling to breathe. Every bullet had been a mule kick to his body. He felt mortally injured, bulletproof coat or not.

"Help me...make things right..." Caelin wheezed. "Help me kill'em all."

McConnolly instead frisked and disarmed Caelin.

"Only God can make this right, brother. Eternal hellfire awaits ya for this slaughter."

CHAPTER 35

Daemiana frantically yanked and clawed at the bars until her hands bled. The familiar bang and swoosh of silver bullets outside meant one thing: Inquisitors. She had to escape! How was it possible? Were not the Inquisitors dead? Had more arrived so soon? Did they kill Caelin? Would they soon find and kill her as well? Daemiana paced the cell, desperately scrutinizing every bar from top to bottom, looking for a crack or flaw or weakness or anything which could help lead to escape. Nothing! Not a spec of rust, not a blemish of any sort on the cold, dreary irons. How could this have happened?! Caelin was supposed to have been different! She had been a fool to remain with him so long and let down her guard! Males had to be used and discarded before they could hurt or betray her! Why had she thought that he would not let her down like every male before him? Never again would she allow herself to repeat that same mistake—

A jolt of agony dropped her to her knees. It had begun.

"No! Please! No!" she pleaded with herself, trying to will it away.

The nightfall's insidious full moon racked her innards. She screamed as her bones crackled and ground and tore at her flesh and skin from inside, extruding slowly and stretching her out as coarse hairs sprouted like weeds from her pores.

"I refuse!" she screamed.

Daemiana dug her nails into the concrete floor. She fiercely resisted the shapeshift by grasping desperately within herself for the will to stop or slow it somehow. Her mind was assailed by visions of her Coven brethren welcoming the shift with glee while she instead sobbed with anguish. For she and her Coven brethren became one and the same beneath the full moon, bound together tightly by the cursed pact, united and desiring only one thing: to hunt and kill as a pack. On such a night, when the full moon torched overhead, they were all one again.

Her mind was invaded by visions through the Alpha Werewolf's eyes:

The orcas were ramming the ice, still intent on blood. Beneath the full moon, Dionisio was fully, uniformly, and swiftly shifting. He towered 11-feet, with muscles more heaving than that of any grizzly. He let out a booming, diabolical roar that shook the ice and echoed for miles.

A massive orca pounced onto the ice, undeterred, and tore into Dionisio's side. It thrashed violently, trying to maul Dionisio in half.

Dionisio ripped into the orca with his own jaws while pounding and clawing its skull unrelentingly. The orca — unable to drag Dionisio back into the water or escape — squealed as Dionisio continued mauling and pounding and clawing its head until Dionisio crushed its skull and ripped out its brains. Dionisio gorged while Cybilia howled up at the moon, her legs fully regenerated.

Two other orcas furiously breached the water and smashed down on Dionisio and Cybillia, knocking them off the ice and into the sea. The killer whales battered them with their flukes. Out of nowhere, another orca rammed them full speed, head-on, launching them high into the air, cartwheeling over the water surface like limp seals.

Dionisio and Cybilia crashed back down into the water with a big splash. The werewolves countered-attacked with a barrage of claw strikes as the orcas resumed mauling them. Dionisio tore into an orca's jaws, gripped its tongue, and ripped it out.

Cybilia clawed out another orca's eye.

Dionisio then tore into the alpha whale and ripped into its blow-hole, burrowing his claws deep into its flesh. The orca frantically dove down into the depths, taking Dionisio with it. Dionisio tore deeper and deeper and deeper into the killer whale until eventually resurfacing with its heart in his jaws.

The orca pod retreated in defeat.

Dionisio and Cybilia pounced back onto the ice and howled diabolically at the moon. They then turned their diabolical sights to Kreuger Sound.

Bloody tears were streaming from Daemiana's eyes as she sobbed, still fiercely resisting the shapeshift. Dionisio was alive and on his way back. She would soon be hunting and killing alongside him again, at least for one more night, before he resumed trying to kill her the following day. They were ultimately slaves to the pact, never that more apparent than on the night of a full moon when hunting and killing as a werewolf pack was their only plight.

CHAPTER 36

THE GUN WAS WEIGHTY AND CLUMSY IN IVERS' PARTLY-FROSTBITTEN hand. His other hand was clutching a blood-soaked flashlight he'd pulled from the muck. His weary forearms were cross-locked, aligning his aim with the beam's sanguine hue as he stormed the jail, gnashing his teeth to mute the arthritis smiting his every joint, which had been fully stoked by a tumble mid-descent amid the mountain's whipping, subzero gusts. There'd be no traversing the local peaks again and surviving. The agony of every step told him so, as he navigated the dark like an old turret, gyring slowly, readying to unleash hell on anything lying in wait. Ivers' final mission was coming to an end, one way or another.

Beaudry and McConnolly limped along behind him, swords in hand, dragging Caelin by the arms. The toll inflicted on all three slayers by the mountain had been unsparing.

Ivers hit the switch on the wall.

"Lock him up. Then, we'll hunker down in the chapel for the night," Ivers ordered. "He is in God's hands now. Steel bars won't stop the Coven."

The jail lights finally flickered on.

Ivers' eyes widened at the sight of Daemiana locked in one of the two cells, keeled over and resisting her transformation with all her might.

"Jesus..." Ivers rasped. "Keys. Now. Move! Move! Move! Before she shifts! We have one final chance at ending this right!"

They ransacked the jail, seizing the ammo as they went. Ivers located and grabbed a large key ring, then hurriedly unlocked and opened both cells. McConnolly tossed Caelin into the empty cell and locked him in while Ivers and Beaudry burst into Daemiana's cell and pounced on her. McConnolly then rushed into Daemiana's cell last and locked the cell door behind him.

Daemiana kicked and screamed, more than half-transformed. They pinned her down.

"Begin the Romanum Execution!" Ivers ordered.

They pressed their silver swords against her body.

The searing hisses and her bloodcurdling screams jerked Caelin back into consciousness. He slowly pulled focus through the bars and watched Ivers tear off and shred Daemiana's crimson cloak.

"Repent, feral darling!" Ivers demanded. "You are damned unless you repent!"

"Don't kill her, you motherfucker!" Caelin screamed.

"Watch your mouth!" McConnolly raged while holding down Daemiana's legs.

"Repent!" Ivers again demanded of her. "Now!"

"I will NEVER..." Daemiana snarled. "...beg any male's forgiveness. Not yours, not Dionisio's, not Satan's, and not God's!"

Ivers solemnly crossed himself, sighed, and recited in Latin: "Forgive me, Lord. For failing to break the cursed pact, for failing to emancipate their unrepentant souls. Via this Romanum Execution, hell awaits them, if it is Thy will."

"No!" Caelin screamed, knowing the time had come. "You promised to save her soul! You fucking liar!"

"This is your Goddamned doing!" Ivers exploded at Caelin. "The spiritual treatment would have secured her repentance and allowed us to emancipate her soul — ALL OF THEIR SOULS — if not for your interference!"

"Do it, Monsignor! Execute her!" McConnolly demanded.

"The Church mandates the saving of every soul!" Caelin ranted, remembering that much. "You can't do this! You fucking heretic!"

The words cut deep.

Ivers glared at the fucking boy, yearning so badly to hurt him, to rip out his heart. Caelin had brought about Ivers' downfall and was now condemning him for it.

"Hell awaits us both," Ivers rasped morbidly in reply.

Just then, the jail shook as Dionisio tore through a wall, sending the busted cinder block rubble crashing against the opposite wall.

"Now, Monsignor!" McConnolly screamed. "Kill her and cast'em all to hell!"

"You're murdering her soul!" Caelin cried.

Ivers thrust his sword through Daemiana's heart, then drew his dagger while squelching his own sobs. His plight to rescue the Coven's souls, including Isabella's, who was already in hell because of him, had failed. He and Isabella would not be reunited in heaven as he had fantasized for decades, as unbiblical as the notion was. There'd be no righting his worst wrong. His personal crusade was over.

Ivers slashed Daemiana's throat.

"I'll fucking kill you!" Caelin wailed.

Ivers' hatred of the boy crescendoed. He watched Daemiana choke on her own blood while gleefully relishing the boy's agony. Caelin had cost Ivers' the love of his life. Ivers finally moved to cost Caelin's his.

"Finish it!" McConnolly screamed.

Dionisio, Cybilia, and Mikaela charged and tore into the cell's bars, bending the irons.

Ivers began cutting off Daemiana's head. Not before—

Daemiana fully shifted, yanked an arm free, and landed a thunderous claw strike to Ivers' head, sending him headfirst into the cell's rear wall.

Beaudry and McConnolly evaded Daemiana's claw strikes by jumping back.

McConnolly dove forward and descended upon her face, sword blade-first. She rolled aside, evading McConnolly's deathblow, which showered the cell with sparks as the blade gouged the concrete floor.

Daemiana then jumped to her feet, dodged Beaudry's sword strikes, and ripped into the side of the cell so fiercely, the bars bent wide enough apart for her to squeeze through, into the adjacent cell with Caelin.

Caelin stumbled back. She pounced at him, intent on devouring him. Caelin leaped aside, scrambled past her, and dove through the bent bars into the opposite cell, landing at Beaudry and McConnolly's feet. Just as—

LeVee tore through the cell's rear wall. He ripped his claws into McConnolly and yanked him out of the jail. Beaudry dove and grabbed McConnolly's arm.

Amid the chaos, Ivers regained his senses. He stumbled back to his feet, clutching his throbbing head beneath the armored hood of his armored coat. Outside—

LeVee sank his claws deeper into McConnolly's armored coat and tore him from Beaudry's grasp.

Ivers watched helplessly as—

McConnolly shot and stabbed LeVee defensively until able to break free and scramble back to his feet. But LeVee tore McConnolly down to the ground again with inhuman speed, more viciously than last time, intent on devouring him.

Ivers and Beaudry took careful aim with their guns. They opened fire on LeVee.

In the cell, Caelin frantically grabbed Ivers' sword off the floor. He jabbed at the werewolves tearing through the cell's bars. Outside the jail—

LeVee was mauling McConnolly's leg, undeterred by the silver bullets ripping into him. McConnolly's leg finally snapped as he hung from LeVee's jaws, upside down. He twisted and turned in desperation, screaming in agony. He managed to grab onto one of LeVee's massive legs, then thrust his sword into the leg's Achilles tendon, severing it. LeVee's leg buckled, and they both crashed down to the ground.

McConnolly crawled away toward the chapel while LeVee shrieked and thrashed about, unable to stand.

Back inside the jail, the other werewolves' onslaught collapsed the cell, pinning Ivers, Beaudry, and Caelin.

Beaudry slithered out from beneath the irons. He jumped back to his feet and fended off the werewolves with sword strikes.

Caelin struggled to extricate himself while—

Ivers stared up at the ceiling motionless, pinned beneath the bars, unable to move. He couldn't feel his legs. It was over... He had failed in every way, by every metric. Spiritually. Physically. As a human being. As a man of God—

Beaudry grabbed Ivers by the coat and yanked him out from beneath the bars, back onto his feet. Ivers screamed in excruciation while Beaudry resumed fighting back the werewolves.

Ivers grasped at the frayed ends of his will to remain standing. His hip was blown. The scalding agony pulsed up his body as he teetered forward and drew his dagger. His beloved Isabella awaited him.

"I am the Grand Inquisitor!" Ivers roared and locked eyes with Dionisio.

Dionisio leapt over the swivel of Beaudry's blade. He crashed down upon Ivers, pinning him beneath his crushing weight while Mikaela and Cybilia tore into Beaudry.

"Grand Inquisitor," Dionisio snarled.

"I am," Ivers proclaimed while weakly thrusting his dagger into Dionisio's neck.

Dionisio clawed Ivers in an unrelenting blur of demonic rage until Ivers' armored coat was in bloodied tatters and inter-mangled with his flesh.

Caelin finally extricated himself from beneath the collapsed cell.

Mikaela pounced on Caelin.

Daemiana busted out of the cell and knocked Mikaela off Caelin, trying to devour him herself. Mikaela ripped into Daemiana, unwilling to share the spoils.

Cybilia knocked over and pinned Beaudry face-up. He shielded his face from Cybilia's onslaught with his arms while wrapping his legs around her massive torso as best he could. He jerked aside to dodge her death blow — which ripped into the concrete floor — while repositioning his legs upward and locking them around her huge shoulder. Beaudry clamped his body against her monstrous arm and clasped her claw with both hands in a swift, fluid motion. Cybilia viciously slammed Beaudry into the concrete floor, over and over, as Beaudry cranked the armbar tighter and tighter by contorting his torso far back with all his might, hyper-extending Cybilia's elbow further and further until it snapped so violently, her fractured arm bones ripped through her furry skin.

Cybilia yowled while Beaudry drew his dagger and repeatedly thrust it into her stomach to further weaken her. He let go, fell at her feet, and slashed her Achilles tendons, finally dropping her. Beaudry then yanked his sword off the floor and hacked past her claw strikes and laid merciless siege to her throat with his blade as—

Dionisio ceased his attack on Ivers and pounced at Beaudry to save Cybilia.

It was too late. Cybilia's shrieking head rolled off her body as Dionisio crashed down upon Beaudry and clawed him unrelentingly. Beaudry attempted an armbar on him as well. Dionisio — too massive and powerful — lifted Beaudry up high with ease and slammed him headfirst into the concrete floor so viciously, it left Beaudry too stunned to defend himself. Before Dionisio could kill him—

"I've killed more of your kind than you will ever of mine!" Ivers growled.

Dionisio slowly turned, foaming at the mouth with rancor.

Ivers was again on his feet, somehow. His tattered coat and flesh hung from him like twined, silver-laced beef. Blood was pooling at his feet. Only at journey's end could Ivers admit his second greatest life regret.

"How I wish could have slain you too, Alpha Wolf," Ivers said to him.

Dionisio charged.

Ivers thrust his dagger into him with all his might.

All regrets dissipated. After decades alone in the gray, on the hunt, joy deferred, dreams forsaken, all for a greater good, at a better place, in another life. It all made sense again. He'd only been wrong about his final destination. He would soon be reunited with Isabella — in that *other* place.

Dionisio's claw had ripped through Ivers' chest and out his back. He lifted Ivers, held him eye to eye.

"You failed to break a single one of us, Grand Inquisitor," Dionisio snarled. "You failed to break the pact."

"I'll see you in hell, Dionysus..." Ivers promised him. "I will slay you there."

DIONISIO BIT OFF IVERS' HEAD.

Ivers' soul drifted into eternity while his blood spewed.

The steely red rained down on Caelin while Mikaela and Daemiana battled over him.

Dionisio suddenly ducked a swooshing blade to the back of the head. Beaudry then ducked Dionisio's counter-claw strike while cocking his sword for another swing but was struck by Dionisio's opposite claw, which thrust him into Daemiana and Mikaela. The two ceased mauling one another and pounced on Beaudry, along with Dionisio.

Beaudry curled up within his armored coat while the three werewolves ravaged him.

Caelin crawled away to escape.

The werewolves turned on him, allowing Beaudry to scramble for the exit as he swiped his sword and dagger off the floor, seizing the chance to escape.

Caelin dove through the hole in the jail wall, hit the ground outside, rolled onto his feet, and sprinted toward the chapel. He swiped his dagger and ice axe off the ground as he blew past his pack.

LeVee was crawling after McConnolly, and healing fast.

Beaudry yanked McConnolly up, threw his arm over his shoulder, and helped him flee toward the chapel.

Dionisio, Daemiana, and Mikaela were gaining fast.

Caelin closed in on the chapel.

Beaudry and McConnolly turned and opened fire while stumbling backward, slowing the werewolves enough to have a chance at reaching the chapel.

Caelin ran up, yanked open the chapel double doors, rushed in, and locked the doors behind him. He stared at the sanctuary lamp while the unrelenting gunfire and diabolical growls drew nearer and nearer. His trembly hand hovered over the door lock. He wasn't about to let the Inquisitors in. But he couldn't let the werewolves win outright either. The battle had to be dragged out long enough for both sides to continue killing each other, Caelin decided. So he unlocked and flung open the doors before he could second-guess himself.

The slayers dove in while firing outwards.

Caelin shut the double doors and locked them again.

He turned slowly and faced the Inquisitors with dread, knowing there was nothing to stop them from killing him. But they had bigger problems at the moment.

McConnolly clutched his mangled leg as Beaudry scrambled back to his feet, reloaded and holstered his gun, then checked his holstered sword and dagger.

The werewolves clawed at the chapel doors to the sounds of charring hisses and backed off.

Beaudry was pacing around and screaming in a frenzied rage, "My God! Why hast thou forsaken me?!"

The werewolves' booming roars engulfed the chapel.

"Out of the depths I cry out to thee O Lord!!" Beaudry ranted, looking increasingly unhinged.

Caelin backed away from it all and wiped Ivers' blood from his face.

"They...killed Ivers..." he sighed to himself, laboring to get the hideous sight out of his mind.

Beaudry rushed Caelin and flattened him with a punch to the face, then kicked him in the ribs.

"*You* killed Ivers! Like you killed this town! Like you killed your own father, you faithless coward!" Beaudry fumed vitriolically, having finally snapped and broken his vow to speak only in biblical passages.

On the floor, Caelin swung his dagger at Beaudry's shins in furious retaliation, then thrust his ice axe at Beaudry's balls with his other hand as he stood, barely missing each time.

"I will fucking kill *you*!" Caelin promised him.

Beaudry slowly drew his sword to kill him.

"Not in the chapel!" McConnolly groaned while wrapping his broken leg.

Beaudry instead backed away and disappeared into the darkness.

Caelin leaned against the wall and slid down to the floor. Beaudry's words had wounded him more than the beating. Maybe because there was truth to them. Caelin's self-loathing smoldered and consumed him. With the adrenaline gone, the agony and fatigue fully set in. His nose was busted and bleeding; he was beyond battered all over. He closed his eyes, on the verge of succumbing to defeat.

"I gotta m-m-make things right..." he rambled quietly to himself over and over.

"ONLY FAITH MAKES THINGS RIGHT!" Beaudry roared maniacally at the top of his lungs repeatedly, as if trying to finish Caelin off with his words. "ONLY FAITH MAKES THINGS RIGHT!"

CHAPTER 37

THEIR CLAWS SCRAPED THE OUTSIDES OF THE CHAPEL WHILE THEIR rumbling moans rattled the walls and all inside. The pitch-blackest corner of the chapel was where Caelin and his ire stewed. He teetered from woe to self-loathing and back again. Caelin was at the end of his line and unwilling to descend any further into the depths of hell. He ignored Lori's choppy wails, too broken to be of any comfort to anyone. She was on the pew where he'd left her, curled up and covering her ears, hysterical with fright, but alive. Caelin was just grateful her blood was not on his shitty, blood-soaked hands too. He couldn't take much more. He was as on the verge of a mental breakdown as anyone.

Beaudry was sharpening his sword on the altar, looking diabolically deranged while angelically Gregorian chanting the Lord's Prayer in Latin.

McConnolly was on the floor, teeth clenched in agony, sweating feverishly, clutching his mangled leg while glaring at Caelin.

"Ya part of this now, brother," he grunted. "Ya own this now too."

Caelin glared back at him, unsure what he meant.

"No one can know what happened here is what I'm gett'in at. As much as this's all your fault, it'll be the Church who'll be disgraced."

"The Church is already a disgrace," Caelin replied.

"Rabid bears did this! Ya, understand?! Those things out there are *rabid bears*! That's what happened here! This ain't the Church's fault!" McConnolly fumed. "Just a tragic, yet natural anomaly. That'll be the official story. The Order'll see to it. Just keep ya mouth shut if ya make it outta this alive. Forget what happened here. Forget us. Cause the Order won't forget ya if ya speak of it. I'll personally come back for ya head! Ya understand!"

McConnolly then grunted and groaned, fighting back the pangs of agony, "Now, ya gonna help us kill those *rabid fuck'in bears* out there!"

So that was why they hadn't already killed Caelin. They needed all the help they could get at that moment. Caelin coolly nodded, having already committed to slaying the Coven with or without them, "I will. But I'll never adopt your guys' aversion to the truth, or for doing *what's right*."

"N' ya have a firm handle on the truth, n' what's right, do ya now?" McConnolly scoffed dismissively.

Caelin glared back at him. He was not going to become like them, no matter what. Dad had been adamant about BOTH believing and doing right in life. One did not go without the other. And Father Wallace had taught Caelin enough Church Doctrine — as a condition of being allowed to be chapel groundskeeper — to know that *Faith Alone* was bullshit.

"You guys conflate Grace and Justification," Caelin said to him. "To justify your moral relativity. While proclaiming absolute truth. You can't have it both ways."

McConnolly's eyes widened and grew incensed, but he offered no denial or rebuttal.

"Ya blind to the truth, brother. The Reformers were right. The Church's Biblical ideals are unattainable; Good Works are unsustainable. ONLY through Faith Alone can we judge those in need of judging, n' kill those in need of killing. Inquisitions and Crusades are best justified that way."

"How can you believe that when it goes against everything?"

"For our Faith is a genuine Faith," McConnolly espoused piously. "God will never lead us astray."

Caelin labored to square the logic, "So...you're *possessed* by God?"

The Coven's deafening howls suddenly boomed, shattering the sanctuary lamp and leaving them in complete darkness. Lori jumped to her feet, screaming and clutching her ears and losing her grip on sanity. Caelin switched on his headlamp, jumped to his feet, and hugged her tightly, trying to comfort her. She shoved him aside and ran for the exit.

"No!" McConnolly screamed as Lori shoved open the double doors and fled before he or Caelin could grab her.

"Oh ye, of little Faith! Run, yes run, lost sheep! Now you too will suffer the tortures of the damned!" Beaudry roared.

Caelin grabbed his dagger and ice axe off the floor and ran after Lori as McConnolly tried to stand but collapsed, clutching his mangled leg.

CHAPTER 38

CAELIN SCOURED THE GROUND ON HIS HANDS AND KNEES. HIS EYES canvassed the periphery as he crawled along until he was sure nothing was coming at him. He scrambled to his feet, prowling along stealthily toward the diabolical growls. He dove behind a decrepit shed. He again looked around. Lori's screams compelled him to jump to his feet and sprint to her full speed.

The Coven was chasing her down as she came into view. The swoosh of their claws cut her down.

"No!" he screamed while charging toward imminent death.

The Coven all turned.

Their glares mauled his soul. Just then—

The anxious neighing and barking of the search-and-rescue horses and dogs emanating from the Sheriff's kennel-barn caught his attention.

Caelin veered his sprint in that direction instead while screaming, "Come and get me! Leave her alone! Eat me!"

He grabbed his pack off the ground as he blew past the destroyed jail, "Over here! Eat me!"

Caelin kicked open the kennel-barn double doors and rushed in, "Come and get me!"

He frantically opened the dog cages and horse pens, releasing them all, except for one horse.

The animals stampeded out of the kennel-barn in all directions, creating chaos and disorienting the werewolves.

Caelin stuffed spare horse bridles and reins into his pack. He then opened the remaining horse's pen as it bucked wildly. He approached it slowly, "It's okay; you're okay."

He calmed it long enough to bridle and rein it.

Caelin hopped on.

It nearly knocked him off as it blew out of there, bucking wildly.

The Coven werewolves had chased down and disemboweled one of the other horses, causing it to trip, slip, and slosh around on its intestines before they tore it apart.

Caelin veered his speeding horse toward Lori, only to realize Beaudry was already there, kneeled beside her. Caelin rode up, his heart sinking as Beaudry closed her eyes while mumbling a prayer.

Lori's throat was ripped out. Her beautiful Nordic nose and high cheekbones, and smooth skin had been mauled into hamburger. The diversion had failed.

Caelin looked away, unable to stomach the sight. She'd been the only girl to be sweet to him, making his life in Kreuger Sound more bearable. He had failed her. More blood on his hands.

A fiery rage consumed Caelin.

"I'M GONNA FUCKING KILL YOU!" Caelin screamed at the werewolves.

The Coven slowly turned.

Caelin locked glares with them.

The werewolves charged.

Caelin's horse bucked and raced away, but not before Beaudry grabbed onto Caelin's coat and leaped up onto the back of the horse for dear life, behind Caelin.

"Get the fuck off!" Caelin screamed.

"Back to the chapel!"

"Fuck you!"

"Do it!"

"I'm gonna fucking end this!" Caelin raged as the horse reached full speed.

CHAPTER 39

Beaudry jammed the barrel of his gun against Caelin's head.

"To the chapel!" he ordered as they neared it. "Stop the horse!"

The gun painfully butted Caelin's head with each bounce of the speeding horse's gallop.

"I'm not telling you again; God damn you!"

Caelin kept kicking his heels harder into the horse, his sights fixed on the open wild full speed ahead.

"I'll blow your fucking head off!"

They blew past the chapel.

Beaudry furiously fired the gun at the sky.

"Next one's in your head!"

"I'm gonna kill'em all!" Caelin raved. "And I know how!"

"You don't know a damn thing!"

"This is my horse! Jump the fuck off!"

Beaudry glanced back as if considering it. It was too late. The four werewolves were quickly gaining on them.

"You just killed us, Goddamn you! Like you did, everyone else!" Beaudry raged. "A horse cannot outrun a werewolf! You imbecile!"

The werewolves were only feet away.

Beaudry took aim back at the werewolves and opened fire, emptying an entire clip into them, then reloading, and again opening fire, over and over and over, until slowing them down just enough for the horse to begin pulling away and to eventually escape.

They arrived at a creek, dismounted, and drank ravenously alongside the horse. Caelin slowly stood and rested his head on the horse's side. The pounding of its racing heart slowed while they rested.

"We can do this... Let's catch our breath..."

"We won't survive the night," Beaudry scoffed. "Not during a full moon."

Caelin stared at the wicked moon's reflection on the water surface as the Coven's howls boomed in the near distance.

"During a full moon, you hide, you hunker down, you survive, if you're lucky."

"I know how to make it back to the river cabin without having to go over the mountains," Caelin replied. "It's super risky, but the horses can make it. Cause at the river cabin is where we're gonna kill them."

"You couldn't kill a cockroach."

"EVERYTHING we need to kill'em is there."

"That's your grand plan?!"

They flinched as a second horse came into view upstream, having somehow escaped the werewolves as well. It too drank from the creek.

"Fine then, there's your horse," Caelin said dismissively and opened his pack and tossed a spare bridle and reins at Beaudry's feet. "Go back to that chapel death trap if you want. *I'm gonna make things right.*"

Caelin mounted his horse and raced off as the Coven's howls boomed closer.

Beaudry — bridle and reins in hand — approached the other horse as it drank from the creek.

Once atop the horse, Beaudry glared in the direction of Kreuger Sound, then in the direction that Caelin rode off. The werewolves' howls again boomed, even closer.

"Goddamned, kid."

Beaudry kicked his heels into the horse and sped off, having no choice but to follow Caelin's lead.

CHAPTER 40

The aurora had slithered into a green whorl and glowed grander than the stars. The feral moon beamed supreme. It reigned in splendor, raging against the sharing of the night. Celestial alliances languished as that tyrannous full moon strained the heavens.

Its luminance waned. It was being outshone by the orange of scattered fires raging below — whipping and jostling and jabbing alongside the Salmon River, not far from the river cabin. The blazes resembled the fires set by Caelin the other night to survive. On this night, the fires were a prelude to blood.

The horses were reined to the cabin hitch post with chains. No one was around. The horses neighed anxiously, growing more and more agitated. They began bucking and shrieking, trying to break free and flee as—

Two monstrous masses were stealthily crossing the river toward the cabin. It was LeVee and Mikaela moving in to devour the crying horses while Dionisio — the biggest, most menacing werewolf —

and Daemiana — nearly as menacing — converged on the other side of the cabin.

Rigged bear traps awaited them, all over the ground, all around the cabin. It was like a bear trap minefield. Dionisio and Daemiana stopped, backed away.

LeVee and Mikaela had entered and were navigating the bear trap minefield, stepping over and around the traps, ravenously moving in on the horses to feed, not realizing the horses were bait—

A bear trap was suddenly thrust down on Mikaela from atop an adjacent tree by Caelin. It clamped onto her head with crushing force, spattering her steaming blood as—

Beaudry did the same to LeVee, from atop another tree. Both werewolves shrieked and thrashed around, unable to flee since both traps were tethered to the trees by Caelin's climbing ropes. As both werewolves stumbled and flailed around, trying to break free, they stepped into the bear traps laid out on the ground. Both werewolves were anchored by the feet as well, trapped, despite their frantic thrashing.

From atop the tree, with his ice axe strapped to his back, Caelin drew his silver dagger, pointed it downward, held the handle tightly with both hands, and jumped. He crashed down onto Mikaela, furiously driving his dagger deep into the crown of her head.

Beaudry followed Caelin's lead and did the same to LeVee with his silver sword.

The werewolves' shrieks boomed for miles as steaming blood gushed from their heads.

"We own the high ground!" Caelin raged.

"This's too unorthodox!" Beaudry replied amid the chaos.

"Just get back up in the trees fast!" Caelin screamed as they extracted their blades and stabbed and hacked at the werewolves' necks, over and over and over, barely managing to cut off their heads and kill them before—

Dionisio pounced on Caelin and ripped into him. Caelin covered his face with his arms as Dionisio tried to tear through his armored coat while—

Daemiana did the same to Beaudry.

Caelin reached for one of the remaining bear traps, slid his hand beneath it, and thrust it up at Dionisio. It clamped onto Dionisio's arm with bone-crushing force as—

Beaudry did the same to Daemiana.

While Dionisio mauled through the steel bear trap, Caelin stumbled to his feet and readied to thrust his dagger at Dionisio's neck. But Dionisio struck Caelin's chest with his other massive claw, sending him flying back.

Caelin slammed into an adjacent tree and hit the ground even harder, semiconscious.

Beaudry jumped to his feet and swung his sword at Daemiana's head. She ducked and countered with a claw strike, sending him flying back as well.

Dionisio and Daemiana broke through the steel bear traps as—

Beaudry and Caelin stumbled to their feet and backed away.

Beaudry drew his gun and opened fire as Dionisio and Daemiana charged. He emptied the clip into them, slowing them enough to reload and do it again and again as he and Caelin backed closer and closer to the shrieking horses.

"This's too unorthodox!" Beaudry fumed, out of his element.

"Hide in the trees after we lose'em!"

"We're not going to make it!"

"Stay near the river! Survive till dawn!"

"It won't work!"

"Stick to the plan!" Caelin screamed.

They jumped onto their shrieking horses.

Beaudry opened fire on the chains, breaking them.

They blew out of there in different directions, on horseback.

Dionisio charged after Caelin, his eyes reddening with fury.

Daemiana pursued Beaudry.

Beaudry glanced back and saw Daemiana gaining on him fast. He veered his horse toward a small boulder. The horse lept over it, and Daemiana did the same. Beaudry then veered his horse toward a downed log but then suddenly veered around it. Daemiana lept over the downed log and landed in a bear trap. It clamped her ankle with bone-crushing force, spattering her steaming blood as she fell to the ground, shrieking.

"You're mine now, bitch!" Beaudry rejoiced as he turned the horse around, drew his sword, and charged.

Daemiana furiously tore through the trap.

Beaudry aborted the attack and blew past her as she jumped to her feet. He sped back the way they came with Daemiana in pursuit.

"Goddamned bitch!"

Caelin blew through the wild with Dionisio swiftly gaining and seconds away from ripping into the horse's ass. Caelin veered the horse toward a tree and ducked as he rode beneath a bear trap hanging from a limb by a climbing rope.

Dionisio slammed facefirst into the bear trap. It clamped explosively, anchoring his head to the tree while his momentum thrust his legs and body airward. The tree limb broke as Dionisio flipped and crashed headfirst into the ground. He flailed and flopped around, stunned, trying to break free.

Caelin turned the horse and drew his dagger. He charged, bent on finishing him.

Dionisio tore through the trap, jumped to his feet, and resumed his incensed charge.

Caelin aborted and veered the horse toward higher ground, paralleling the river, with Dionisio rapidly gaining.

Beaudry was speeding back toward the river. He rode up on the rear of the cabin, slowed his horse, and cautiously navigated the numerous bear traps. He spun the horse around, readying to engage and hold his ground.

"Bitch!" Beaudry screamed, waving his sword.

Daemiana was nowhere to be seen.

Beaudry continued looking around.

Nothing.

There was a swoosh.

Beaudry turned and looked up, realizing Daemiana had lept off the cabin roof.

She crashed down on Beaudry. The force knocked over the horse and sent Beaudry flying out of the bear trap minefield.

The horse rolled onto a bear trap, which clamped shut and anchored the horse to the ground by the back. It whined and shrieked while kicking futilely.

Beaudry winced while lying on the ground; the wind knocked out of him. He regained his senses, scrambled, and dove for his sword, which hadn't landed far. He grabbed it, rolled onto his back, and thrust it upward, deep into Daemiana's chest — to a loud charring hiss — as she again crashed down onto him.

Daemiana tore into Beaudry without relent, mauling at his neck and eventually tearing through his armor. All while Beaudry ferociously stabbed her head with his dagger to get her off him.

Daemiana pounced back defensively, but Beaudry held on to his sword with his other hand, extricating it from her chest as the force yanked him back onto his feet, where he transitioned the momentum into a singlehanded, backspin sword strike at her head.

Daemiana ducked. But her pointy wolf ears fell to the ground, cut off as she barely dodged the sword strike.

Daemiana's eyes reddened with rage.

Beaudry holstered his dagger, clutched his sword with both hands, and assumed his lethal, high guard defense.

She circled him, snarling with diabolic fury.

Beaudry grinned, looking at ease, back within his element, despite his bleeding throat.

"Time to die, devil bitch."

Daemiana lunged forward but aborted as Beaudry's sword again swooshed past her head, his swordsmanship increasingly lethal.

They attacked and counterattacked until—

Daemiana ducked and backward somersaulted over Beaudry's follow-through strike. She landed behind him, ensnared him in her claws, and locked her jaws onto the back of his head.

Beaudry's legs nearly buckled under her crushing weight.

He thrust his sword backward at an upward angle over his shoulder with all his might into her throat. The blade blew out the base of her skull.

Beaudry then spun around as he drew his dagger and slashed her throat, then stabbed her neck over and over like the merciless assassin he was.

She lifted and slammed him down to the ground and mauled at his neck as he continued stabbing hers while shielding himself with his other arm the best he could.

They laid hideous siege on one another's throats, soaking each other in one another's blood.

Daemiana eventually fell over, beside Beaudry.

She crawled away, with his sword still lodged through what was left of her neck. Her head was still attached, barely.

Beaudry was gagging on his own blood.

He managed to draw his gun and opened fire on her neck, attempting to finish severing it. But he was too badly marred to keep the gun steady. He fired and missed again. He again fired and missed, then fired and missed again.

"Die...bitch..." Beaudry frothed and gagged. "Why won't you fucking die? Die!"

The illuming horizon besieged the full moon as—

Caelin was fleeing full speed along a bluff that steeply overlooked the Salmon River.

Dionisio had closed the distance and was seconds from tearing into the horse's ass. His hot, rancid breaths were nauseating Caelin more than the thought of being torn apart.

Caelin finally accepted the inevitable with restrained despair, then veered the horse sharply — over the ledge.

Dionisio leapt after them, sank his claws and jaws into the horse, and hideously ripped it in half in mid-air.

Caelin, Dionisio, and both halves of the horse plummeted and crashed into the Salmon River far below.

Caelin resurfaced eventually, coughing and gasping for air, struggling to swim, tangled in horse guts. He choked down bloody water while cutting through the innards and entrails with his dagger to extricate himself.

Both halves of the horse drifted away, kicking, eyes wide with terror as it slowly died.

"I'm sorry…" Caelin gasped, pleading with the horse to forgive him. "I'm sorry…"

He eventually crawled onto the shallows, then onto the bank, coughing violently, too scared to look up.

He finally did.

Dionisio was standing over him.

Before Caelin could react, Dionisio grabbed him by the neck and yanked him up so violently; he dropped his dagger.

Caelin's feet dangled far off the ground.

Dionisio held him eye to eye, the way he held Ivers before biting off his head.

Caelin looked up pleadingly at the illuming sky, "Faster…"

"No help, Inquisitor," Dionisio rumbled. "No God, only death."

Caelin glared into Dionisio's eyes with a solemn acceptance of any eventuality, "You first."

Menacing grunts sounded nearby.

"Like I planned it."

Dionisio turned to look as predawn was succumbing to dawn. The full moon was fading, and he was slowly shrinking back to his daytime form. The Salmon River grizzlies were emerging from hiding, foaming at the mouth with fury, intent on reclaiming dominion over their river. They ruled the daytime.

The scar-faced bear was the first to charge.

"Inquisitor!" Dionisio roared, realizing Caelin had led him into the final trap.

Caelin cheered on his improbable plan: salvation at the jaws of the monstrous bear that killed his father and ruined his life.

The scar-faced bear smashed into Dionisio, breaking his grip on Caelin. Caelin fell to the ground as Dionisio and the scar-faced bear crashed into the river, followed by the other bears, all bent on Dionisio's blood.

Caelin grabbed his dagger, crawled away, struggling to stand, wincing in agony. He stumbled to his feet and staggered back toward the cabin, away from the swivel of claws reddening the river.

Dionisio was no match for the bears' overwhelming fury. He was overpowered eventually, mauled, thrashed around, and torn apart.

The morning sun's first gleam shimmered in harmony with Dionisio's fleeting shrieks. The river ran red and steaming.

The smoking ash and burnt trees, the singed cabin, and blood-stained ground all told Caelin there was nothing left to kill as he neared, hobbling along, drenched in horse blood, looking like carnage itself.

His hand tightened around the dagger.

Daemiana had come into view. She was lying on her side, her back to him, in human form, nude. Her macabre neck wounds churned his stomach and wrenched his heart as he drew nearer and nearer. She was somehow still alive.

Beaudry was lying nearby, clutching his torn throat with one hand and his gun with the other. He was pale, trembling, near shock.

"Finish her...before she heals," Beaudry gasped.

"Do not give up on me, Caelin..." Daemiana pleaded.

She somehow still soothed him despite everything.

"Cut off her head..." Beaudry ordered.

Caelin's heart sank, torn between what seemed right and what felt right.

"Execute her. Now!"

"I..." Caelin searched for the words.

"The righteous man..."

"But..." Caelin pleaded.

"...liveth by Faith Alone," Beaudry made clear.

"She risked everything. To be free of the curse," Caelin rationalized.

"Kill her!"

"She's the only girl ever to love me," Caelin let slip out in a heartbroken sigh.

Beaudry gagged and frothed and seized violently, unable to breathe, coughing up blood. Caelin stepped closer, only to realize that Beaudry was cackling uncontrollably. Was he laughing at him? He was.

"You imbecile!" Beaudry retched.

"We love each other—"

Beaudry could barely stop laughing long enough to spew, "She doesn't have a cunt between her legs for you to fuck, you senseless moron!"

Caelin struggled to understand what he was getting at.

"It went without saying since she was running around practically naked!" Beaudry raged on.

Daemiana was sobbing, humiliated.

"Accurst abominates, like her and her kind, are asexual!"

Caelin stumbled back, filling with dread, trying to process what he heard. He fell to his knees beside Daemiana and forced himself to look as he slowly nudged open her legs, deeply ashamed over being unable to stop himself. Surely, Beaudry was delirious from his injuries.

"Nature hates them, and that's how nature prevents them from breeding! Beaudry ranted. "It's why Ivers killed Isabella! When he saw! And now that you've seen, you will kill this bitch too!"

Caelin struggled to breathe. The wind felt knocked out of him like never before as he accepted the realization, through his own eyes, that Daemiana had no genitalia at all.

"She's an abomination!" Beaudry screamed.

Caelin filled with rage, feeling conned, deeply disturbed, and humiliated, even though Daemiana had warned him: *I cannot give you what you want.* Caelin furiously punched the ground until his knuckles bled so as not to sob. Love and happiness were just not in the cards for him—

Beaudry's horse neighed and kicked with panic, still anchored to the ground by the bear trap. The bears — drenched in Dionisio's blood — were approaching, eyes fixed on Daemiana.

Beaudry fired his gun into the air as a warning to Caelin and the bears.

"She has no feelings for you because she can't! She's using you! She's incapable of love!" Beaudry raged on. "Kill her!"

Caelin slowly stood, manning-up to his fucked reality. The feminine was always chaos, intricate, perplexing, overwhelming, terrifying, messy, never straightforward or easy. So be it, Caelin accepted with a solemn nod. *Don't be soft. You gotta do, you gotta be strong; that's what be'in a man's all about.* Dad's words had never made more sense.

"She's an accurst affront to God! Kill her now!"

"I'm gonna break the curse," Caelin vowed. "Like Ivers should've done with Isabella. Not kill her."

"How many more have to die before you see that faithless Good Works count for NOTHING?!" Beaudry fumed and took aim at Caelin's face. "Kill her! Or God help me, I'll put a bullet through your Goddamned head."

Caelin just glared into the barrel of the gun.

"I've enough faith to know God can do His own killing. If that's what He wants. I just wanna help others. That's what I want—"

Daemiana pounced as Beaudry fired — with her last remaining strength — and took the bullet for Caelin in the heart. Beaudry furiously squeezed the trigger again but was out of bullets.

"AHHHHHHH!" Beaudry screamed in agony as he rolled toward his sword and grabbed it before Caelin could, then thrust it upward at Caelin's throat, barely missing.

Beaudry found the strength of will to stagger to his feet, wobbly, bleeding profusely from the throat, frothing bloodily from the mouth.

Caelin unstrapped the ice axe from his back. He stood between Beaudry and Daemiana, clutching his dagger in one hand and his ice axe in the other.

"Just walk away," Caelin implored him.

The bears were closing in on all sides, eyes on Daemiana.

Beaudry assumed his high-guard defense, far from top form due to his injuries, yet rabidly bent on cutting down Caelin to kill Daemiana.

"You, like her, were never meant to get out of this alive," Beaudry admitted. "Knew that much the first time I saw you."

"Cause you're a murderer," Caelin replied with no surprise or hesitation. "Not just some hypocrite *rapist*."

Beaudry lunged forward furiously and swung his sword at Caelin's face. Caelin dodged the strike but stumbled back, tripped over Daemiana's unconscious body, and fell. He scrambled back to his feet and charged as Beaudry moved in on Daemiana and thrust his sword at her head.

Caelin deflected the sword strike with his dagger as he slammed into Beaudry, knocking him back and saving Daemiana.

Beaudry spun around and thrust his sword into the side of Caelin's shoulder with such force, it blew partially through the armored coat, into his flesh.

"AHHHHHHHHHHH!" Caelin screamed and fell to his knees, dropping his dagger.

Beaudry yanked his sword out of Caelin's shoulder, stepped in, and swung it down at Caelin's head, but not before—

Caelin thrust his ice axe up into Beaudry's forehead with his other hand.

Beaudry missed, dropped his sword, and fell to his knees, face to face with Caelin — the ice axe lodged deep in his skull.

Beaudry yanked it out.

Blood spewed as his eyes rolled up into his head.

"Death. To the enemies of God," Beaudry gasped, with only the whites of his eyes glaring back at Caelin.

He hit the ground dead.

Caelin also collapsed, spent and in agony, bleeding profusely from the shoulder.

The grizzlies were circling them, snarling, intent on doing to Daemiana what they did to Dionisio.

Caelin forced himself to stand. He was shaky and dizzy as he stumbled to her. He was unable to lift her into his arms. Instead, he grabbed her wrists and dragged her by the arms into the bear trap minefield, navigating the traps until he reached the horse.

The bears drew closer. An outer trap clamped shut prematurely. The bears jumped back, startled but unharmed as—

Caelin lay Daemiana on the horse. He placed his feet on the lower jaw of the bear trap, and using his hands, pulled up on the upper jaw with all his strength, just enough for the horse to tear free.

The horse jumped to its feet with Daemiana lying across its back. Caelin jumped away from the trap as it slammed shut. He then mounted the horse and held himself and Daemiana in place while the horse shrieked and bucked. Caelin managed to calm the horse as the bears again drew closer and closer.

"SSSSHHHHHH, boy..." Caelin soothed while navigating the horse around the bear traps—

A bear charged from the side without stepping into a trap. The horse bolted a split second before the bear tore into it, kicking and bucking.

Caelin held on to the horse and Daemiana tightly, maneuvering the horse as best he could around the remaining traps and bears, barely evading both until finally escaping into the open with the bears in hot pursuit.

The scar-faced bear emerged ahead, blocking their path.

It immediately charged.

Caelin locked eyes with it while kicking his heels harder and harder and harder into the horse, steering the horse straight at it, full speed.

The horse leaped high into the air and over the scar faced bear just before impact.

The scar-faced bear turned and gave furious chase.

The horse pulled away and eventually outran the bears.

Caelin held Daemiana tight in his arms as they again escaped certain death. He choked back traumatized, emotionally spent tears. Exhilaration warmed him against the numbing, subarctic cold. A choppy sigh marked the end of the ordeal. His body and soul some-how still felt intact. He had both believed and had done right by her. It was probably what they called *acting in good faith.* If only Dad could see him now, he'd be proud. Caelin was sure of that for the first time in his life.

CHAPTER 41

The aurora and her shimmery entour hailed the black of a new moon. She and the stars and the heavens mended the wounds wreaked by the full moon. These were the grandest of night skies, for no moon was the only good moon.

A silvery lake was gleaming like an underlying mirror. Up and down were indiscernible, if not for a moment and a rogue ripple. Daemiana stood atop a boulder overlooking the serenity. She was nude, fully healed, and wholly lucid. No moonshine meant no shape-shift — none at all. She was all herself on the night of a new moon as she was all monster on the night of a full moon.

Daemiana closed her eyes, inhaled, cherished the clarity and solace. She recalled her last unfouled night, the night of the last new moon; the last time she had not devolved into an insidious creature of the dark beholden to the extent of the lunar glow. Caelin had not yet entered her life. One moon cycle later, desperation and fear had given way to hope. Daemiana was entirely free, in body, mind, and spirit, if only for this night during this lunar cycle.

Daemiana dove gracefully into the lake. She resurfaced at the opposite end and swam around face-up, admiring the aurora in her untrammeled radiance. Surely, those magnificent northern lights had mitigated the effects of the moonglow, at least somewhat, or so she hoped. Mother Nature's grace was the gift of balance. Daemiana renewed her vow to return to full communion with Mother. Whether or not that uncertainty was to be realized, one thing was certain. On this night, she was beholden to nothing. If only it could be like this always.

She swam out and left the lake.

Daemiana arrived at a nearby hot spring. She watched Caelin soak away the agonies of his many battle wounds. Daemiana entered and sat behind him, gently wrapping her arms and legs around him. The steam permeated and heavied the silence. He had grown dark and distant after the full moon. It had changed him the most, forever perhaps. Things were no longer simple between them. He was as adept a killer as anyone she had ever known. And now, just as emotionally unavailable. The Coven had never been defeated beneath the full moon until it came face to face with his wrath. Caelin had proven himself a mighty and cunning werewolf slayer. But it was not yet over.

"He is not dead," she murmured sensually in his ear while kneading his neck, eventually gliding her hands onto his shoulders and massaging away the tightness there too. His eyes grew heavy and slowly closed.

"He's dead," Caelin eventually replied.

"He is not," she nibbled on his ear.

"I saw..."

"You saw Mother's beasts attack him."

"They tore him apart..."

"Only a decapitating smite to his neck with a silver blade can kill him."

She licked his ear and slid her hand down, wrapped it around his cock, and stroked it until it was hard.

"I will be able to love you fully..." she whispered. "When the cursed pact is finally broken. You must first break and kill Dionisio, my love."

Caelin's bloodshot eyes opened. His rage smoldered over. He swiftly turned and pressed his silver dagger against her throat as if readying to behead her.

"I lost everything cause of you."

"Caelin," she gasped.

"And you're still using me."

"Please—"

"Like the slayers said, you're playing me. You played us all against each other!"

"No—"

"Stop *using* me."

"I am not—"

"Stop lying to me!"

Caelin tossed away the dagger, slid his hands beneath her legs, and caressed her labia.

"There's no curse right now," Caelin fumed, unfooled by her act. He had seemingly reasoned and deduced that beneath a new moon, her genitalia returned.

"I am not lying. I am just not ready."

Caelin nodded with a solemn acceptance, "Just stop lying to me."

"You are not well, you have not been well, and you are frightening me—"

"Scared? I'm the one who should be scared! About being manipulated into another fight to the death with your devil-dog boyfriend!"

Daemiana slapped him, "Do not talk to me that way."

He grabbed her as she again hit him. They wrestled and splashed around in the spring as she kept hitting him. He managed to kiss her while she was hitting him. She gradually hit him less and less while reciprocating more and more. She eventually realized he had released her. Daemiana was free to leave if she wanted. She resumed kissing him.

"I am not ready," she again said. "To lose you."

"You won't."

What she feared was Caelin letting his guard down.

"This changes nothing..." she gasped as his finger entered her. "I will kill you beneath the moonshine."

Her legs were spread, and his cock was in her before better judgment could douse their passions. His thrusts were hard and deep, and the pleasure pangs consumed her. His grunts were as loud as her moans. Her fingernails clawed his back — perhaps a prelude of what awaited him. No amount of love for him would counterbalance or mitigate the feral moon.

Though on this fleeting new moon, Daemiana loved Caelin in body, mind, and spirit. But that love would wane each night until entirely fading away as the lunar cycle progressed. So be it.

Was not love an innately painful, messy, ruinous, and impermanent leap of faith? Perhaps they could work out a happier outcome, one moon at a time.

THE END